the outgoing man

Glen Neath was born in Sheffield in 1965. He
has been a painter, night-club manager, film-maker
and playwright. He lives in London and this is his
first book.

The Outgoing Man

GLEN NEATH

LONDON

Published by Portobello Books Ltd 2005

Portobello Books Ltd
Eardley House
4 Uxbridge St
Notting Hill Gate
London W8 7SY, UK

A CIP catalogue record is available from
the British Library

9 8 7 6 5 4 3 2 1

ISBN 1-84627-000-6

www.portobellobooks.com

Designed by Lindsay Nash
Typeset in AldusBQ by
Avon DataSet Ltd, Bidford on Avon, Warwickshire

Printed by MPG Books Ltd, Bodmin, Cornwall

for Lizzie

Hello. How are you? You've made yourself at home already. I see you've found the most comfortable seat in the house. You've made a beeline for the most comfortable seat in the house. Good.

There are actually many reasons for not choosing the most comfortable seat in the house, as I'm sure you know. For a start it says to me that you're a particular type of person. What sort of person do you want to be?

You don't want to tell me.

And another reason: you have nothing left to look forward to because now you'll never be happy with any other seat; the rest of the seats are as good as useless.

Clearly nothing had any bearing on your decision to sit in that seat. You sat in it. Fair enough.

Something else has just occurred to me; I'm sorry I seem to be stuck on this same train of thought, but give me a moment, I'm almost finished with it.

What has just come to mind is this: did you look around and choose that seat as the most comfortable seat in the house, or did you sit there purely by chance? In which case I'm making all sorts of rash judgements about your character before I've even had the chance to get to know anything about you.

You don't want to talk about it? You don't mind me making all sorts of rash judgements about your character?

What's your name by the way? And how long have you been sitting there?

You haven't got a drink. What would you like to drink? I haven't done enough to make you feel at home. You haven't got a drink, and you're very quiet. Is that through choice? I mean: are you playing games with me? We've established that you aren't shy, after all you sat in the most comfortable seat in the house, so am I right to presume your silence is some sort of tactic? Well it's not working.

And you're sitting there in your coat. You're not going anywhere so why don't you take your overcoat off? You might think you look comfortable, that might be the impression you're trying to give me, but I can see you're rigid as a board under that coat.

And what about that look on your face? You're terrified. You don't think so? What would you say it was then? You're nervous. Of course you're nervous, I'm nervous.

Maybe you're just shy. You don't look shy though.

Maybe you sat in that chair without looking around for anywhere else to sit.

To be honest with you, I wasn't expecting you so soon. That's the problem. You see, I'm not ready for you. Why don't you go out and come back in again?

No?

Maybe you're tired. Are you tired? How far have you come?

So I wasn't ready for you. I've only just finished my packing. Here's my case, look. It isn't much, is it? Everything I own after all these years is in here. Everything else was here when I got here.

How long have you been sitting there by the way? Have I asked you that already? Did you answer me?

I wasn't expecting you for at least a couple of hours.

Listen, you haven't got a cup of tea. Would you like a cup of tea? What about something stronger? You probably made a mental note of where the kitchen was the second you walked in, didn't you? Everything you need is in there. I made sure it was all stocked up as soon as I knew you were on your way. The last thing you want when you've come all this way is to be thinking about buying groceries.

How did you get in by the way? Did I leave the door open? Did you knock? Maybe you knocked and I was upstairs. Maybe you knocked and I didn't hear you because I was upstairs packing. I might have left the door wide open I suppose, and you walked straight in.

You walked straight in. You made a mental note of where all the facilities were. You sat down on the most comfortable seat in the house, by the fire. You put your feet up on the pouf; I would normally ask you to take your shoes off by the way. You probably took a look round the place, the ground floor at least, and maybe you heard me upstairs, moving about.

Was I humming? Was I humming? I often hum when I'm in my own world. What was I humming?

How long have you been sitting there, if you don't mind me asking? I've already asked, I know. I was hoping I might trick you into giving me an answer.

Maybe you've only just arrived, a few seconds before I came in. You look settled though; maybe you're a quicker settler than I am, I'd be sitting on the edge of my seat until all the pleasantries were out of the way, I can tell you, but you might be one of those people who can relax at the drop of a hat. I envy you that.

You must have been wondering what the place was going to look like. Maybe it's turned out to be exactly what you expected. I can't remember what I thought. It seems like such a long time ago. That's what makes it harder to go now; I've been here so long.

Okay, so I'm a bit apprehensive about my future. I wonder what's in store for me. Once I'm through that door that's it, there's no turning back.

Are those my directions you have in your hand by the way? I recognise the white envelope. I remember when I arrived here as the incoming man, I sat in that chair, over there, the uncomfortable-looking one, I sat on the very edge of it, and the outgoing man entered with his case, as I have just done – he wasn't ready for me either – and I had an envelope like that one for him. He took it from me but he didn't say a word. I didn't get the kind of welcome I'm giving you, I can assure you. I don't think he said anything to me at all. We're all different, I suppose. When it's your turn you might say I spoke too much.

Anyway he took the envelope and made a dash for the door. Yes. I say a dash, but it was more like a slow run or a fast walk. He must have been worried about all the same things I'm worrying about now. Where am I going? What's going to happen to me? You might have been wondering what was in store for you too, but you're here now and that's that. For me everything's unknown. I don't know where I'm going to end up.

So that's probably what he was worrying about, when I arrived. And everybody deals with things differently: I can't stop talking, but some people clam up. He was obviously one of those. In fact I know he was because, although he didn't say anything to me at the time he obviously wanted to, or wishes he had, because I heard from him very soon after. He got in touch a couple of weeks later by mail. The postman delivered a postcard. And I must say I was very surprised because he hadn't been in my thoughts at all since he'd left.

I said to the postman, 'Who gave you this?' And the postman said, 'What?' Of course he said, 'What?' Then I brought the card inside and put it on the table and couldn't look at it.

The picture on the front was of a large hall, like a village hall or a ballroom, with wood panelling on the walls and a colourful print of a volcanic island above it that stretched the entire length of the room. On the tables around the dance floor there were lamps in wicker baskets. The room was full of people. They were dancing.

On the reverse the card contained all the news of the progress he'd made since leaving me, and I considered it an indicator of the sort of things that were in store for myself. That's why I read it, in the end. It said: I feel I ought to begin as I mean to go on, but I'm crippled by the thought that you won't read anything I write. If you get it you might read it or you might not. You might not get it. It's a leap of faith.

He went on nevertheless, he wrote: I often cast my mind back to our meeting, you know. I remember I spent hours preparing for your arrival. I had the whole thing worked out. I'd planned to give myself time to sit in front of the fire before you arrived, with my feet up, listening to the King's College Choir singing Allegri's *Miserere*, or Mahler's Adagietto from *Symphony*

Number Five, or something on Radio 2. I was going to leave the curtains open while I waited for you; I thought a warm light would draw you in. But you were already waiting for me, weren't you? You arrived while I was busy upstairs, bathing and shaving and shampooing my hair, and dressing and packing, and using my last minutes to reminisce about some of the moments I'd spent up there over the years bathing and shaving and washing my hair.

I was disappointed to see you, but only because I wasn't expecting you so soon. My plans were suddenly made obsolete.

We stood there face to face for a minute or so, do you remember? Neither of us said a word, it was a chance to gather our own thoughts I suppose you could say, a moment spent in isolation, each to our own contemplations. But then I suddenly noticed that a bad feeling had come between us and I was mystified as to the extent of it, you see it seemed to have sprung up between us so quickly.

I suppose you could say we got off on the wrong foot. With the benefit of hindsight maybe I resented you because you had obviously settled in so quickly. And to make matters worse, you were waiting for me to break the ice. After all, wasn't I the man of the house? Wasn't I the one who was supposed to do all the talking? Well, I'm not much of a one for talking, as you have probably gathered. I remember thinking to myself though, Shall I ask him if he'd like me to draw the curtains, which was quickly followed by the realisation I shouldn't be asking you – me, the outgoing man, asking you, and you the incoming man, and not even properly in at that, at least not properly in until I was properly out.

You know, what I would really have liked was for us to have simply crossed on the path, me as the outgoing man and you as the incoming man; and then for the briefest second, while we were abreast of each other, we would simply be men.

But that was not to be. The whole thing was a mess, to be honest. But it's impossible to go back and change anything.

Believe me though, right up until the final moment I wanted to call out.

In the end I said, 'good luck', or maybe I didn't, I thought I had but there was no response from you, so maybe I only thought I'd said it. Anyway I told myself I'd said it. Whatever, it came from the heart. And I told myself, in the weeks that followed, that you'd taken my words on board, that you'd understood the intent with which I'd said them, and the feeling I'd imbued them with; and I'd said them with feeling because at that second I had meant it, and had it not happened at that moment that I instinctively meant it, I would have strived to mean it, because I knew all too well that moments like that are rare.

That was when I decided to write to you. Because I thought

I'd missed an opportunity and I began to think about how you would react when your incoming man finally came along. You'll feel the same responsibilities towards him that I felt towards you I'm sure, only you'll make a far better job of welcoming him in than I did.

I suppose it comes down to this: what would I want you to say about me?

Well, you've heard the things I've said about him. Now I'm thinking about the things you might say about me when your turn comes. Say that I welcomed you, at least. I want to tell you everything now, face to face, because human interactions are few and far between. Say that I had no such human interaction when I arrived.

He wrote, and he wasn't into his stride yet: Before I go on in this vein, I would like to apologise in advance.

Ha!

I declare to you now: the account I give, of my journey from the house, will be full of holes – embellishments to the truth if you like – but any I make I make only to clarify the plot: for example, I might move an incident backwards or forwards in time for the sake of a more pleasing composition, or I might erase a character who unsettles the plot-line or who I would otherwise judge peripheral to the story. Any encounter that does not further my journey, physical or spiritual, will be dispensed with, or I will never get through everything. In any event, when I attempt a manoeuvre like this I will try and add a footnote to this effect.

Further to this, let me also tell you that whilst I have decided to keep you informed of my progress, I will not be attempting to charm you with stories of any heroic adventures, because I want you to believe this to be a true story, and there will be obstacles enough to that without my inventing more.

But how shall I begin?

What I can tell you is this: I have seen the sea, and it is as it says it is in the textbooks, that is, it is at times blue and at times grey, depending on the state of the sky above it, and it moves first in and then out, or out first and then in, incessantly. And it is just as beautiful as I ever imagined it would be. And a further thing I can tell you is this: I have seen the desert and it is as empty as they say, and when the sun goes down it is as cold. And another thing I can tell you: I have seen the hills and they do indeed go up on one side and down on the other.

Do you know, I have never thought of myself as a person comfortable with travelling, yet I travel light, like someone born to it; my lack of luggage, though, does not come from a wealth of experience, but from a lack of belongings; I only have the clothes I am standing up in, two shirts and some underwear, toiletries and a simple travel alarm clock. I also have a stack of postcards, all of the same view; and what a ridiculous view, eh? I have decided I will only look at the picture on the front of this postcard if I am allowed to look at it with envy, because I've never really liked dancing, although I've always felt the loss of it; I like to watch other people dancing to make up for it. Look at the men in the picture, standing around the edges of the dance floor in the semi-darkness, out of the reach of the spotlight; they watch the others dancing and perhaps even call out the odd instruction. And it is with these men I most closely associate myself, I imagine that maybe, when they return and lean on the bar with their pints, they like to refer to themselves and each other – the other men on the periphery of the action – as supervisors. It is with these men I am happiest. I am not a dancer. I don't want to be a dancer.

If only I could talk to you from the heart. If only I could reveal something of my innermost thoughts. Let me see what I can come up with. When I was finally able to turn my back on you, it was easier to leave. And when I stepped outside the house it was like I was being born. I found myself on my hands and knees on the path outside wailing my heart out, you might have heard me, but after a while, when I realised this was getting me nowhere, when it dawned on me there was no going back, I got to my feet and I walked to the gate, where I opened the envelope you had given me. And after I pocketed the packets of money, given to me in various currencies, I followed the directions contained therein: I went to the station in Neefoundland as instructed, and I bought a plane ticket out of Neefoundland to Thiland, which was to constitute the second leg of my journey, to be taken later on; and I also bought a train ticket to The Footlands, with the expectation that when I got there I should travel by road to the town of Sole – and this comprised the first half of the first leg of my travels; the second half of the first leg was the return journey that brought me back to Neefoundland (in time to make my connection to Thiland).

So as you can see, the second leg of my trip was to be much shorter than the first leg, which was somewhat fractured and was to be made up of many individual parts.

I couldn't help but feel it one journey too many though, this round trip through The Footlands to Sole and back to Neefoundland. I asked myself, why not stay in Neefoundland until it is time to make my connection and not bother going to The Footlands and back at all, but put my feet up and drink coffee instead, or read the newspaper, or a good book, I have one in my case that I didn't list on my inventory to you (I don't know what it is I haven't read it I won't read it you're probably not interested I will never finish it I will never start it that is why I forgot I had it with me but having said all that maybe I left it behind).

Of course the point of the trip to the town of Sole was that there'd be things there I'd have to assimilate, that would be required to inform the second leg of the trip, because, apart from knowing the name of my final destination, the journey itself was shrouded in mystery.

Meanwhile it began to rain as soon as I was out in the open. I spent a lot of time looking for shelter, a doorway or a bus-stop, and I suppose that was pretty much the course of the first week, the drizzle, standing in a doorway looking out, a meal here and there, eight hours of sleep a night.

On the morning of the day of my first journey, by train, what with one thing and another, I felt unexpectedly optimistic. I had a spring in my step. I had had a very good breakfast: cereal fried eggs toast beans pork sausages bacon blood pudding fried tomatoes fried bread fried mushrooms freshly-squeezed orange juice croissants real butter jam ground coffee.

I also met a man at breakfast who wished me well.

'Your travels,' he said to me, 'are only just beginning.

'I can see by the look in your eye, and the tread on the soles of your shoes that you haven't been very far before.'

Whereas his travels, he assured me, had been long and far-reaching: he told me he had walked across the Sahara, climbed some of the world's highest peaks and sailed across the Atlantic Ocean single-handed in a biscuit tin.

Luckily I was able to just sit and half listen and eat my

breakfast and drink my freshly-squeezed orange juice, because he was only really interested in listening to his own voice; and at the same time I could also half listen, perhaps with the other ear, to the sounds of the canteen: the plates on the trays, the trays on the metal shelf and the almost indiscernible sounds among all of this, of the food surrendering the serving spoon for the plate, and the plate for the gullet.

Anyway I don't think I opened my mouth at all, except to shovel in fried eggs; I think I might have nodded when he first asked if the seat opposite me was free and I shook his hand when I got up to leave, but that was the extent of it.

He was up shit creek without a paddle when I just got to my feet – the legs of the chair screeching on the lino made him shut his mouth for a moment – and in the pause took his hand and shook it vigorously, before picking up my tray and departing the sinking ship. The last thing I saw was him looking down at his breakfast as if eating it was going to be one challenge too many. He hadn't had his cutlery in his hands the whole time I had been sitting opposite him.

I walked out into the pale winter sunshine with a smile on my face. I followed the road that ran parallel to the sea until I came to what looked like the Town Hall and then I turned left, and after travelling inland for a few minutes, I came to the station.

In the twenty minutes I had to spare before boarding my train, I drank a strong cup of coffee and ate a pastry in the station bar and I shat in the station toilet. In the twenty-minute delay while I sat on the train, I looked at my hands on my knees.

Now, while on the train from Neefoundland to The Footlands, which is connected to Legland, but only just, and has influences from all the surrounding countries and capital cities (and in particular from Cnut, famous for its mount, its valley and its dense forest, as well as for the fact it was named after the Danish-English King who was the first and the last to breach its defensive walls), I had a feeling of anxiety that grew by the minute: namely that I would not make it back in time to meet my connection – I mean the flight I had bought to take me from Neefoundland to Thiland.

Was I already worried about this before I had even set out? Probably. That's how I remember it. And I also wondered and worried why I had started on this trip in the first place, a question I can probably answer later.

In fact I always feel anxious when embarking on travel of any kind. Okay, I am being carried over the land by one means or another; I feel giddy, I feel I have been extracted from myself, and I speed along like a ghost without my feet touching the ground. And I also questioned where I was headed for: the name of the place is only a name; it offered me nothing solid to hold on to.

Along with this and any other questions, I also had rebellious feelings. What am I doing? I thought.

Then I thought, okay then, no, I won't do it. I'm going to get off the train and find my own way to the Promised Land, and by that I don't mean the land promised to me in Thiland, I mean another Promised Land, a Promised Land of my own choosing, and I left room for any suggestions as to where that might be.

But one Promised Land, I thought straight after that, was the same as any other Promised Land in the end and I realised I had no preference.

So then it occurred to me to sit down and go nowhere, yes that's it, I thought, I shall go nowhere, but where to sit? I would have to find a place to sit.

I soon decided I would get bored of sitting before I got bored of moving about.

Then it was too late for either option because the train was moving.

As a method of calming myself I counted on the timetable the minutes out from Neefoundland, where I was starting from, and where I had to make my way back to in order to make my connection, and then I subtracted them from my departure time at the other end (in The Footlands), so that in order to make my connection, I would know how long I would have to leave myself to make it back, if all ran smoothly on the way back in (smoother than it had so far been on the way out), and then I added a few minutes for good measure in case for some reason I was held up, and then I added on a few more minutes in case I wasted the few added minutes, I don't know, eating or walking or looking at the sky, or for a bout of diarrhoea or a debilitating headache, and then I set a time in my head as the latest time I could safely leave The Footlands to return, in time, to Neefoundland to make my connection, and I made a note of it on the back of a till receipt (for the coffee and pastry) and placed it in my wallet.

The fear then, of missing my plane in particular and of everything else in general, grew not by the minute, but by the mile, and I decided a formula could be conceived, whereby the distance travelled and the time taken could be directly related to the anxiety I felt, but even this became negligible as my anxiety suddenly and surprisingly began to diminish with the comforts that the journey provided: seats that reclined, the inspiring countryside that passed by outside the train window; the climbing land and falling clouds, the cacophonous sky, the impending rain, the sun impending beyond that and the clear sky and the impending dark sky when the sun closed its yellow eye; at once rolling landscape dotted with houses, or high banks that suddenly and surprisingly obscured the rolling landscape and the dotted houses dotted on it, or short tunnels that suddenly and surprisingly obscured the high banks, and then more rolling landscapes out of the other end of the short tunnels, and sometimes more houses dotted on the rolling landscape, and sometimes nothing but woods and trees and rivers and earth and the expectation of nothing by that earth but the receiving of everything greedily: the rain to feed the grass to feed the cattle to feed the farmer and his wife, and the following sun to dry the rain, and the tractor wheels that scar the soft ground.

At some point, in the midst of all this, we reached the border that separated Neefoundland from The Footlands, but only in name, because all outside the window seemed the same.

And when sitting in the carriage and not looking at the rolling landscape dotted with little houses or the high banks or the short tunnels, I was reading the directions I had been given, and was forced to constantly remind myself of the three things I had been told were of importance when encountering the new country of The Footlands, namely: 1) that Lipland is not Lapland; 2) that The Footlands is not in the Balkans (and neither are Lipland or Lapland for that matter); and 3) that even though, when viewed on a map, the shape of the province (including Thiland, Neefoundland and The Footlands) may resemble a headless chicken running eastward (when the city of Cnut and its irrigation system – like the spokes on a half bicycle wheel – is to be the freshly-severed neck spilling its freshly-spilled blood, the mountains to the north to be a clump of tail feathers, and the towns of Upper and the southern-most Sole to be feet), it is in fact hurrying in the opposite direction, namely westward in its aspirations, economic and cultural.

Northern Mountains

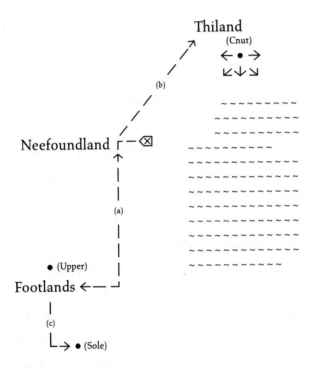

Thiland
(Cnut)

Neefoundland

(b)

(a)

● (Upper)

Footlands

(c)

● (Sole)

(a) travel by rail
(b) travel by air
(c) travel by road

Then underneath the important points 1), 2) and 3), the further, and equally important instructions, that read: A) go to The Footlands (and from there to Sole); B) meet X; C) get directions to give to the outgoing man ahead of you in Thiland; D) give X in The Footlands news about the incoming man behind you in Neefoundland; and E) get a response from X in The Footlands about the outgoing man ahead of you in Thiland and the incoming man behind you in Neefoundland, if, and only if, X feels like giving one, otherwise leave it at that (the rest unsaid); and F) return to Neefoundland and make your connection as already instructed in the previous directions, which you should already have burned; and oh G) burn this set of directions as well, when the mission has been accomplished.

First, then, I had a few things to consider, namely: a) when was the mission considered to be accomplished – when I had made it back successfully for my connection, or when I had made the initial contact and got the required response? (And what was the required response, and did I need to know that? And would I recognise it when it came?) Or, to go back to the first point, is the mission accomplished enough when I have made the initial contact? And incidentally, how long was I expected to wait for a reply before deciding X was going to remain tight-lipped, and b) a further incidentally: how am I to know whether X is a he or a she? Or rather, and this ties in with a) – that being, whichever (he or she), how am I to recognise them? And c) I shall think about c) later, for now I am wrapped up in a), b) and all the subsequent subsidiaries of a) and b) recently unearthed.

I feel I am getting lost in my own meanderings. Let me tell you a bit about the people I encountered on the train. A woman with a very sad face – so much so that I think she was putting it on for effect – asked me for a few of the local coins to buy a ticket, or else the guard was going to put her off the train. I had none. She spent a lot of time looking at me so I decided to avoid her by taking a pee. The guard sneezed on me as we jostled in the corridor, where he was punching tickets. I queued behind an elderly lady, only it turned out she was in early preparation for alighting at the next station and not wanting to relieve herself at all. Meanwhile a woman with a small child pressed by us both, me and the old woman, this queue that wasn't a queue, and disappeared into the vacant stall with the child, but the child either couldn't pee or couldn't evacuate itself, or never wanted to in the first place, and the woman obviously would not let it get up until it had done one or the other, but whatever the story, they didn't come out. And because I didn't want to leave my bag unattended as the train pulled in to and out of the next station, I went and sat back down, and thought I would watch for the woman passing back, with the child, outside my compartment – but then it occurred to me that they might have got off the train as well, the child with its trousers round its ankles perhaps and the woman dragging it by the arm.

The woman with the sad face had moved on, for now at least.

Then the customs official appeared – this was just as we sat in the stationary train astride the border (I don't know whether I was in the half of the train that had its foot in Neefoundland or the other half that stood in The Footlands) – and he checked my passport and he checked the passport of the woman in the carriage with me and then he asked me, 'Have you anything to declare?'

And I said to him, 'Yes. Aren't we all obliged, at some point, to make our own way in the world?

'And isn't it also true,' I added, 'that no one wishes any other of us any harm?'

He didn't speak, which encouraged me to continue.

'And let me further push home that point,' I said, 'by announcing I am willing to stand up and say that we are only burgled, or killed, or raped, or held at gunpoint, or held at knifepoint, or touched up, or abused (verbally or physically), if we are in the way of the burglar, the killer, the rapist, the gunman, the knife-wielder, the pervert, the verbal or the physical abuser getting what he wants, i.e. our money and possessions, a sense of power over somebody else, or his "kicks" – be they got through the wielding of guns and knives or raping or buggering. I mean to say that all of these things are motivated not in order to make us, the victim, feel worse, but to make him, the perpetrator, feel better. We may as well be somebody else or a hole in the ground for all he cares.

'I am sure, incidentally, that there are exceptions,' I added swiftly, 'perhaps I can think of an example.

'A Mr Jones, who lived down the road from me when I was a child and a teenager,' I said, 'received a note in the post, which at the time was just a note, until a second note came, and then it was the first in a series of notes and the whole thing was about to take a turn for the worse. For now, though, the first note was a seemingly innocuous scribble, a simple and short message, something along the lines of: Are you a Mr Smith? And do you live at the address as indicated on the envelope? Please reply to PO BOX etc. etc. And Mr Jones, taken with curiosity as to the identity of the mystery author and his seemingly genuine and generous tone, replied: I am not he, I am a Mr Jones. Who are you? And how did you get my address?

'And with that the mystery man had the name now, as well as the address, and soon enough the letters began arriving with monotonous regularity, and they got much, much worse.

'But of course, as I'm telling you this now,' I said, 'it has just occurred to me that the story of Mr Jones might not be an example of an exception to the rule after all, because while it seems the perpetrator is acting only to make the life of Mr Jones hell, he may in fact be acting, not out of any malice towards Mr Jones at all, but for purely selfish reasons, that being, he likes to make another human being feel persecuted (that may be how he gets his "kicks") and the victim may as well be somebody else, another victim, or a hole in the ground for all he cares.

'Perhaps it is plain for us all to see now, with hindsight, that instead of continuing his search for a Mr Smith, he quickly and probably quite happily transferred his attentions to our Mr Jones. And again, moving sensibly on with this line of reasoning, can't we also presume one of these two conclusions: either he considered his options and decided it easier to persecute Mr Jones than continue to search out a Mr Smith to persecute, or alternatively, he was never looking for a Mr Smith in the first place. Either of these explanations only further illustrates the point I have been trying to make.

'But as an adjunct to that,' I said, 'let us also not forget that Mr Jones suffered anyway, for years and years, until finally they arrested an old man who lived in the village, who was once headmaster and then a governor of the local school, and who, upon retiring, found himself bored sick and out of his mind, and who took to delivering hate mail to anyone he knew or could remember or could get to know through subterfugenous methods (such as the one he used in the first instance on Mr Jones), in order to relieve himself. And it was only the good grammar and the Latin in the notes that gave him away in the end, and also the fact that Mr Jones's initial reply was returned to him, marked with a number out of ten in red ink in the margin.

'But it is also important to note that Mr Jones did not know this man to begin with,' I continued. 'No. And he still did not know him when the whole affair was finally over and done with and the man was in custody. The man had merely been a sudden and unwelcome intrusion that came to govern many of Mr Jones's movements here and there and might have sent him to an early grave. I say might have, because I do not know what became of Mr Jones in the end, I only know what was happening to him at the time, when I was a child and a teenager, and even then I only knew what was happening to him through the second-hand mouth of my mother and the words she spoke to my father (which I suppose meant they reached me third hand, a further hand removed, and entered into my, at first underdeveloped and then uninterested, teenage ears). The words were never intended for me at all then, but I listened to them anyway, often from the top of the stairs – you see I had inherited my father's ears, and he and his whole family were known for their ears for miles around, and it was almost impossible not to listen in to clandestine conversations from time to time with ears like I had.

'Anyway, the facts of the Jones case,' I hastened to add, 'if they have been at all embroidered, have only been embroidered slightly, to better illustrate my point, the point I have been trying to make, which is that a decision you perhaps make here, today, could have a resounding and rebounding effect somewhere else tomorrow, and I ask you to bear that in mind, and you might think that is obvious, but so is the nose on my face, and I take after my mother for her nose, and her family, who were famous around those parts for their noses around that time. As far as my eyes go, I have no kind of eyesight worth talking about, good or bad, and neither had the families on my mother's side or my father's side. I did though have a friend at school with 20/20 vision, and he did most of the seeing for me that I wasn't able to do myself, and if he needed any hearing or sniffing doing I would happily return him the favour.'

And I almost felt that I would leave it at that, my declaration to the customs officer, when I noticed that the woman in the carriage was looking at me and so I carried on talking to – what? A) impress her (what indication did I have that she was even impressionable…?), or B) not allow myself a moment to be alone with her because a) I could not trust myself, or b) I could not trust her, or c) neither of us was to be trusted, or C) I suddenly found I had something else I wanted to say.

'Although I am not a happy traveller by nature,' I said, 'that is I do not like to move when I cannot feel my legs doing the moving under me, it feels however as if this elongated period of inertia, sitting here on the border of neither here nor there, is going to kill me. Can't we get moving again? Do you understand? At least while we're on the move my mind can't dwell for too long on any one thing.'

I closed my eyes. When I opened them again they were glazed over a bit, and I realised I had turned my thoughts in on themselves: I was considering, I think, how I might get the woman into bed. Where did that come from? It had, after all, had to barge its way through all the anxious thoughts about moving and not moving that were filling my head. What a lovely looking woman. I looked out and saw through the thin film of dew in front of my eyes that she was still sitting opposite, and now she was smiling at me.

The customs officer abruptly turned and left, as if in a huff. Maybe he understood, in my language, only the words he had spoken, namely, have you anything to declare? And also perhaps yes and no and hello and please and thank you and can I have a glass of beer? and all the obvious things you learn to ensure you can get by when in a foreign country; but of course he was the native and I was the foreigner. Maybe he was sensitive to the frisson between me and the woman, the woman in the carriage with me who suddenly said, 'I would just like to say I agreed with everything you said.'

I said, 'You haven't taken your eyes off me. And what beautiful eyes,' I remembered to add (I wasn't a fool).

And she said, 'Let me show you the sights.'

We hit it off immediately. I told her I loved her, I said, 'I can say that while we are here, in limbo, on the border between Neefoundland and The Footlands because I am bound by no laws after all, that I know of, and I can forgo any obligation to the customs and traditions of either or etc. So, I love you and or etc.,' I said.

'It's too hot on this train,' she said. 'While I may be instantly attracted to you, the heat has made me lethargic and I am unable to act on it.'

'Oh.' I got to my feet. 'Let me open a window,' I said.

'No!' she called out.

'What about taking off your hat and gloves and muffler?'

'No!' she said again, with equal vigour.

'I suppose we have the rest of our lives,' I said, and I sat back down. 'What would you say to that?'

She told me that she would never hurt me, just as I had made reference to, in my speech. No, she would never harm me knowingly and promised me as much (which was a weight off my mind from the off), and while she might hurt me soon enough, I thought, at least I would find some comfort in the knowledge it wasn't something she had against me in particular.

We inched forward into the station. Everything and everyone were obviously in order. I carried her bags off the train. We ate in a bistro in the Town Square, where I had the local delicacy and she did not. I felt immediately at home here and she was delightful company; when she laughed I laughed. Actually I saw it as my job to make her laugh.

I woke up later, in that following night, beside her, and listened for her slow breathing. I couldn't hear it. I climbed out to pee. On the way back I kicked the travel alarm clock I had placed on the floor beside the bed, under the bed, and it clattered against the far wall. I struggled on my hands and knees to reach under the bed for it; I knew it was going to ring at some point and it was better to struggle under the bed for a silent clock than a ringing one. Anyway while I reached for it I must have grumbled, or groaned, as there was a painful twinge in my right shoulder. I lay in the bed beside her again after that, and listened for her breathing. I thought the palaver with the alarm clock might have roused her but there wasn't a peep, there hadn't been a peep. I lay stricken, not breathing, waiting for the slightest sound.

Then there was silence for six months.

There was no word from him and I had no means of contacting him either. He finished with, that's all for now, I'll drop you another line soon. *Well. And then nothing else for six months, not a line, not a dropped line.*

Would that constitute a cruel act, would you say? What would you do under circumstances like that? You'd probably make up some stories of your own, wouldn't you?

So what do you think I did? I did just that, I imagined his route I imagined the woman. But before I could get very far with it I began to care less and less about him. He was like the hero in a novel I might have read once, or a distant relative I had never known. And when the postman brought a second card I almost didn't bother reading it. It lay on the kitchen table for a few days before I picked it up absent-mindedly – ha – while I was spooning sugar onto my cereal.

First I noticed it wasn't the same view as before on the front, as I'd been expecting; it was a view of the sea. My curiosity was aroused enough to pick it up. It was the sea all right, and it was a perfect blue-green with boats sailing on it and a strip of land down one side, which interested me less.

After looking at it for a few minutes I turned it over. I recognised his handwriting immediately, it said: Sorry it's been so long since you heard from me, but shortly after my previous correspondence I fell into a black mood and certainly couldn't write anything, and then shortly after that I suddenly found myself in a good mood and I was enjoying myself too much to put pen to paper. I can speak about it now though because I am confident I have levelled out, I have neither the terrible black thoughts I once had nor the joyous ones that followed them.

I can't remember though, where I left off: had I conducted

my business in The Footlands as ordered, and returned to Neefoundland as directed, in order to go to Thiland as told to do in the original letter of instructions?

I will only say that the strange land known as The Footlands is only a distant memory now. And the land Neefoundland, where I left you, where I started out from, is stranger and more distant still. I have settled down here – and I am now at the heart of things – and it doesn't seem strange to me at all, although it seemed a little odd when I first set foot in it. And I can tell you I am about as happy as I can be, considering the circumstances.

But I'm getting ahead of myself. Am I right in thinking I was telling you about the woman I met on the train? Well, she was gone in the morning and so was money from my wallet, the bitch. And I have little to remember her by except that I had been very taken with her. Her name was Emily. I remember she called herself Emily because I told her that was my mother's name. She was very accommodating and she had an unexplainable tattoo on her hip, I'd asked her what it was of and I'd kissed it, but it remains a mystery to this day: I think, with hindsight, it might have been a warning but I couldn't read it – if only I'd concentrated on languages in school.

Due to the fact that I had woken up and was half awake during the rest of the night, she was probably able to slip out in the morning, fully rested, without waking me.

Anyway, whatever happened, that next morning I found myself on my own; at first I had no idea of where I was to begin looking or what exactly I was supposed to be looking for, if I was supposed to be looking for anything at all. I considered sitting in my hotel room and awaiting contact from them but I gave up on that idea almost immediately, and I wandered around the city for a few terrifying days with my hands in my pockets, looking for a sign. I watched the faces of the people that passed me in the street, and I saw in every smile a moment of complicity, but nothing came of any of them. I met hundreds of eyes across numerous crowded rooms but none of them lingered long enough to suggest anything to me.

I started to look in shop windows at the cards advertising this for sale, or requesting this in exchange for that, or offering rented accommodation, and I began noting down numbers and letters, hoping to somehow crack the code, but nothing indicated itself to me, even though in the evenings I laboured over the digits and letters for hours, putting them first in order in a straight line, and then running them vertically down the page in the hope that inspiration would come to me suddenly.

One day I even followed a man, who seemed to be moving as if he knew I was behind him – which seemed to me to be invitation enough – from the Central Square into the suburbs and then onto the scrubland at the edge of the city, where he sat down in the long grass and masturbated over a magazine he had been carrying with him in a plastic bag. I moved around him in a wide arc, just beyond the fringe of his vision, which was sorely restricted as a result of the intense focus he was applying to the shiny pages; from the back, hunched over and at a distance, he looked like the stump of an old tree, twitching slightly, perhaps trying to uproot itself.

On my way back I waited for the bus and saw something in one of the numbers, I can't remember what, I can't even remember the number, but I waited for it hopefully, letting two number 14s and a 21, I think, go past. My bus delivered me back to the Central Square without incident.

I returned to my boarding house totally demoralised; I had already criss-crossed the city a hundred times.

The weather had become oppressive over the course of the weekend and I planned to sit in my room until summer returned, or spring. I decided I would at least stay put until there was a feeling of optimism in the air once again.

I think it was at this time I decided to write to you, but I was lost to black thoughts and a sense of futility and couldn't put pen to paper.

When I was lying on my bed like this, one day, in a black depression, I suddenly felt a wave of panic sweep over me – I felt an icy hand in among my entrails, stirring them about – because I realised I couldn't recall how long I had been in The

Footlands, and I couldn't bring to mind what day of the week it was or what month of the year, and I had no idea when I was supposed to leave The Footlands to go back to Neefoundland in time to make my connection.

The woman in the local grocery store told me what day it was and the date, but her ability to speak my language was limited and I began to mistrust her.

I frantically began a search of my luggage for the ticket that was booked for the plane that would carry me to Thiland as instructed – somehow though, I recalled I had made a note some time ago and put it in my wallet for safekeeping, I had a clear picture of doing it in my mind. I scrambled around, looking for my wallet, finding it eventually in the back pocket of the trousers I had left over the back of the dining chair. I immediately went to the place I had placed it, clear as this action had been in the vision I had had, and I found it and opened it and the writing on it, in a hand I didn't recognise, which wasn't my hand, said, Go to the Central Square and catch a bus, a number 28, and go to Sole (a borough) and get off at the main junction on the High Street.

You can imagine; I sat back on the bed for a long time with the scrap of paper in my hand and wondered what had happened, and furthermore, when it had happened. I began to have the uncomfortable feeling I was being watched, and although I was also elated that finally there had been some recognisable contact, I was also alarmed that this had been able to happen under my nose, because I knew I had been vigilant. I had never been more vigilant. Every day, every minute I had been in the city I had spent watching for some kind of sign, and I had had no contact with anyone, I had been careful not to touch anyone or let anyone touch me.

I thought long and hard about how the note could have got into my wallet; after all, hadn't I slept every night with the door locked, and I considered myself a light sleeper and knew I would have been disturbed by any member of the staff with a skeleton key entering my room in the night; in fact hadn't I slept with the dining chair wedged up against the door handle?

And the only conclusion I was finally able to reach, after hours and hours of deliberation, was that Emily, the woman on the train, had placed the note in my wallet when she took the money out of it, on the night I first booked into the room, and of course that raised all manner of more despairing thoughts still, as I remembered all the fruitless days combing the city, unaware that I had the further instructions already tucked away inside my wallet in the back pocket of my trousers.

I almost couldn't bear it, and it was only the hint of what the note might lead to, the anticipation and trepidation as to the instructions I had been given, that stopped me losing hope altogether.

I also wondered (and worried) if the instructions were still valid after all this time (that is, if what I had surmised were true and Emily had been the courier), but what could I do now but follow the instructions to the letter and hope for the best?

I read the note again; the letters were lazily formed, the 'a's looked like 'u's, but I hadn't misread it, it was clear enough. I put it to one side. I took a glass of water from the tap and sat on the bed. I drank it down in one and put the empty glass on the bedside table. I remained sitting on the bed. I looked at my hands on my knees. Although they weren't shaking they had taken on the identity of a stranger's hands. I think perhaps they *were* shaking if I'm honest, but I would say my head was shaking simultaneously with them, in fact my whole being was humming.

I concentrated. I even closed my eyes. I thought about what I should do. It was no use rushing out now, into the night, I decided. Instead I planned to be up and dressed and out of the hotel first thing the next morning, without breakfast, without even the sip of coffee I always insisted I needed to get myself going, and from here I would walk quickly to the Central Square.

I pictured the scene: it would already be very cold and not yet properly light. I would touch the wallet in my back pocket from time to time as if I was expecting somebody to take it from me although I wouldn't have passed within ten feet of anyone since leaving my room, in fact wouldn't I, if I saw someone approaching, fear the worst and cross the street, and at one point wouldn't I even step into the entrance of an arcade, still locked up for the night, and wait for the coast to be clear? I would find the bus-stop, probably on the eastern side of the Central Square and read on the sign the number (which by now seemed like a strangely magical number) of the bus, and see that it did indeed go to Sole (a borough), and that it went through the suburb of Upper (a borough) on the way, and passed close by where I had ended up when I followed the man with the magazine.

That made me feel I'd already come close to where I was going, by accident. (I remembered, rather fancifully no doubt, that I'd noticed something in the air at the time, a thickness.)

And I imagined a man would probably be there to meet me at the bus station in Sole, and his special powers would include the ability to make me feel at ease and we would laugh and joke for a time until he was ready to deliver me to X, who in turn would be the most charming man in the world.

On the back of these pleasant thoughts of course, there came despairing ones. I was, after all, at the edge of the unknown.

I didn't have too much time to think about it though, because there was suddenly a knock on my door and I didn't get a chance to say 'come in' before the door opened and a man was standing there.

He was quite a big man, bigger than me. Actually he was

only mid-height, I saw when he stepped over the threshold, with mid-brown hair and ordinary features. His teeth were his main distinguishing characteristic because they were so badly broken and discoloured. His cheeks and neck were red as if the cold air outside had irritated his freshly-shaved beard. He had mid-brown eyes (or hazel, is it?) and a blue suit on. The neck of his shirt was open. At first it never occurred to me it was me he was looking for.

'Hello,' I said, 'what can I do for you?'

He moved towards me and introduced himself. We shook hands.

He said that I was to go with him. I asked what for (I still didn't have a clue) and he said, 'To see X.'

I asked him if he was sure, and he nodded and said, 'Yes.'

I was to get in the car with him and he was to drive me.

I said, 'How far is it from here?' And he said he couldn't be sure, but that it was reachable.

I was very aware that we were standing face to face like this and also that I suddenly didn't want to go after all.

'I need to pack,' I said, to stall for time. 'Why don't you sit down and I'll make you a cup of coffee?'

But he seemed rather agitated and wanted to stand while I got my things together. I wanted a few moments though, and I put the kettle on anyway.

'It won't take me a minute,' I said, 'I haven't got much, but I need a second or two, I wasn't expecting it to be hurried like this, not when the time came.'

'I understand,' he said and made the concession of sitting on the dining chair. I put my case on the bed. After I had made the coffee I went to the dressing table and put my toiletries away. While I packed we made small talk.

He said his name was Mr Brown, and that he had been in X's employ since he had left school at sixteen. I said, 'What do you do for X?'

He said, 'This and that.'

'Since you left school?'

'I'm thirty-four,' he said, but people say I look younger. What do you think?'

'Yes,' I said. He did. All the features on his face were rounded, he had a pudgy nose and his eyes were large, a combination that conspired to make him look more like a boy than a man.

'People say I look about twenty-eight,' he said. 'People have said I look twenty-eight ever since I was twenty-eight and now it seems I'm stuck with it.'

'That isn't so bad,' I said.

'Says who?' he asked. 'Says you?'

'Yes.'

'Thirty-four is a good age,' he went on, 'but twenty-eight is not.'

'Oh.'

'I woke up on my twenty-eighth birthday and was stricken with self-doubt and self-loathing,' he said, 'and since then the whole of the world has been against me.'

'I don't believe it,' I said.

'Believe me you don't stand a chance.

'Let me give you a piece of advice,' he added, 'avoid twenty-eight at all costs.'

I told him it was all behind me. He said he was surprised, that I looked younger. I said no.

He said twenty-eight had been a bad year for everyone he knew: his sister had met with an unhappy accident in that year, and his brother, who had been trying to give up smoking because he was afraid of cancer, finally succumbed to a melanoma on his little toe, which was promptly amputated.

I said he just needed someone to break the pattern. He said yes. I told him twenty-eight had been one of my very best years. He said, 'Yes, it's either very good or very bad I suppose, it's one or the other.' He sat very stiffly in his chair. He didn't unbutton his jacket. He sat like this, all buttoned up, while I continued to pack my things in my case.

'I was just considering the instructions I was given,' I said finally.

'Hmm,' he said in reply. He obviously had no interest in talking about it; he was in his own world, really.

'What is X like?' I asked finally.

'He's a fine man,' he said, and to prove it he said, 'Let me give you a for instance. I used to know these two guys,' he continued, 'and they were best friends at school.'

'Was one of them X?' I asked.

'No,' he said. 'I'm getting to that. These two men were the best men at each other's weddings,' he said, 'and when the time came they were the godfathers of each other's sons. I loved that kid as though it were my own.'

'"I"?' I interjected.

'What?'

'You said "I".'

'Did I?'

'Yes.'

'He,' he went on, 'I meant he. *He* loved the kid as he loved his own,' he said. 'And they spent a lot of time in each other's houses, you know, because they lived next door to each other.'

'Yes,' I said.

'But one day one suspected the other of having an affair with his wife. I don't remember where the suspicious thoughts came from, there wasn't any incident as such that I can recall, it was more an intuitive feeling: the wife's eyes might linger too long, you know, when the neighbour came round, or the neighbour, over a round of golf with the husband, might, at the mention of the wife's name, pause involuntarily and for the briefest possible moment, and demonstrate a faraway look. But it was enough and his swing might have been affected.

'Then one day, matters took an unexpected turn for the worse when one of the kids, the older boy, the son of the cheating neighbour, hit the other one, the son of the husband and the unfaithful wife, on the nose, in the school playground; they were supposed to be arguing over a girl or something. And of course I hit the roof.'

'"I"?' I butted in again.

'I?' he said, 'did I say "I" again?'

'Yes,' I said.

He pondered the situation momentarily and then he took out a cigarette and lit it.

'Let me get you an ashtray,' I said.

When I sat back down he didn't go on, he sat deep in thought. Finally I said, 'What happened?'

'What?' he said.

'What happened with the two men and the two boys?' I asked.

'The trouble between the boys was an opportunity for the husband to express all the anger he felt at the betrayal of his wife with his neighbour,' he said.

'Yes,' I said, 'I can imagine.'

'In truth the boys themselves had all but forgotten the incident. It's interesting, don't you think, that the man was unable to question his wife or his neighbour directly?'

'I suppose it is.'

'Perhaps he didn't want to know.'

'Maybe not.'

'They were in the garden one day,' he said, 'each aware that the other was over the fence but not speaking to one another, and what with one thing and another, and the things that remained unsaid, they ended up rushing inside, grabbing a knife each from the kitchen drawer, and setting about one another. I stress though that it wasn't brutal, it was strangely civilised. It was like a fencing match.

'Anyway the wronged husband, the father of the wronged boy, was wounded, which just goes to show you there's no justice in the world. And the neighbour called for the doctor. I think the treacherous wife was inside, I think they were alone, the two men, you know, when it all went down, or the wife would surely have tried to come between them.'

'So it was the neighbour who called the doctor?' I asked.

'Yes. But that doesn't make him a hero.'

'No.'

'Emphatically not,' he said.

He sat and drew on the cigarette until he put it out on the saucer I had fetched for him in the absence of an ashtray. Then there was another silence. I thought the story was over. It didn't look as though he was going to say anything else.

'What if I don't want to go with you?' I asked, rather tentatively.

'What do you mean?'

'What if I don't want to go?' I repeated.

'I'm to make you,' he said.

'I can make it there on my own,' I said, 'if you tell me where to go.'

I wondered whether I could take him. He looked over-sized again, now he was sitting down, he looked big, when for a second or two I'd thought he was mid-sized. I tried to recall what he had looked like when he was standing up. Then I considered the physical state I was in, I had been sitting around for days now after all, I'd taken a few walks perhaps, but I knew I wasn't prepared for this kind of encounter, while he was probably honed, he was probably prepared for it twenty-four hours a day. It was his job to be ready. He looked ready.

'You're coming with me,' he said, as if he'd been reading my mind.

'Sure,' I said, 'whatever you say.'

This time he unbuttoned his jacket, as if with my acquiescence he was able to relax a bit, and he took out the pack of cigarettes. He lit a second one and after taking a long drag on it, he put his hand on his knee again, this time resting the back of it against his leg with the cigarette in his cupped palm.

'Anyway,' he said, 'after the man was recovered from his wounds he met his neighbour at the garden centre. Out of the blue the neighbour said it was never the right season for marigolds, that marigolds were vulgar in some way, that they were weeds. It touched a raw nerve because the other was a big fan of marigolds. Truthfully though, it was more than the marigolds. He'd have been the first to admit that the situation with the boys had never been put right. And he also felt that the affair between his neighbour and his wife had never even been brought up, never mind put right (although he wondered if the whole thing wasn't over by now, judging from the reaction of the wife to the neighbour and the way the neighbour reacted in the presence of, or at the mention of, the wife).

'Anyhow one thing led to another and they set about each other with the hoes and spades, and the husband of the cheating wife was wounded again. The neighbour again fetched help, this time in the shape of a garden centre attendant, who in turn fetched the doctor, who shipped the man off to casualty to have the gash in his head from the spade stitched up.

'I'm not going to go into it too deeply,' he said, 'but I will tell you that this sort of thing went on for some time.

'The man who was wounded, now on four separate occasions – the affair, the skirmish between the boys (let him also take some of that pain on board), the first battle with the knives, and now this, the second encounter with the hoes and spades – seemed unable to get the better of the other one. I fear it was something to do with the way he was approaching the situation. I think with the benefit of hindsight these are the sorts of assumptions we can make. Anger, while a fine way of raising the bottle enough to enter the fray, is also a great spoiler of the aim. I think his anger wasn't honed in any way. It spilled out of him indiscriminately, while the neighbour's mind was unclouded, because he thought they were fighting about something else, I don't know what, but certainly something that had none of the same emotional charge.

'Anyway in the end the whole issue was resolved by the interference of the boss, who had somehow got to hear of it.'

'You mean X?' I asked.

'Yes,' he said. 'You see they both worked for X, and the man who was doing all the wounding was transferred while the other, the wounded man, was told to stay put. So you might say I had the last laugh.'

'You said "I" again,' I said, somewhat dispassionately, for by now I guessed he was talking about himself.

'Did I?'

'Tell me,' I asked. 'It was you, wasn't it?'

'You've rumbled me,' he said. 'Yes it was me. I think I was embarrassed to confess, you know, because I had succumbed so often.

'Anyway,' he said, 'all this went on when I was twenty-eight.' Which I suppose was like the full stop being placed at the end of his previous assertion, about the unlucky number twenty-eight, I mean.

'Yes,' he said as an afterthought, 'X is a fine man,' before he fell silent again.

The cigarette continued to burn, shielded as it was from even the threat of wind, but remained unsmoked in the cup of his hand.

'I need to use the toilet before we go,' I said finally, after we had been sitting in silence for some time.

He said, 'Sure, where is it?'

I said, 'It's on the second floor.'

He said, 'I'm coming with you.'

I said, 'If I was going to try and escape I could go out through the window.'

'I'm coming in the stall with you,' he said.

I told him I had a shy bladder and I couldn't pee in public.

'It's not negotiable,' he said.

Anyway it was all a game to me. Somewhere inside me there was the voice telling me that I could do what I wanted, that I could go with him or I could go it alone. In the end it was just enough to know it was there, this choice, and I didn't have to act on it; after all, I thought, this man had come a long way to find me and take me back when I hadn't managed to get there by myself.

'We need to get going,' he said.

'It's ten to seven,' I said as I put the travel clock in my case, 'how long will it take us?'

I turned and looked at him because he had said nothing. He was still sitting with his hands on his knees, the butt of the cigarette gone out in the cup of his hand, his gaze fixed somewhere in the middle-distance.

'Let's leave at seven,' he suddenly said.

'What?'

'Let's leave at seven. Seven is a lucky number,' he added.

'Is it?' I asked.

'Let's leave at the time that will be most fortunate and we shall get there safely.'

He turned and looked at me.

'Seven is lucky,' he said, 'but not if you times it by four or add it to twenty-one.'

By now I was at a loss for what to say.

'By rights you shouldn't be adding any numbers together at all,' he said, and he seemed to be miles away by now, lost in his own thoughts, 'especially numbers beyond nine,' he went on, 'because as soon as they become double figures they're weakened. No, if you're after the big numbers you're better off multiplying the smaller ones than adding,' he added.

'Multiplying is more powerful than adding. You see with adding you're bringing one thing to another and making a total out of the sum of the parts,' he said, 'but with multiplication you're making something out of nothing. It's not the sum of the parts, it's the result of a magical process.'

He dropped the burnt-out cigarette butt on the plate and brushed the ash off his hands.

'You're interested in numbers,' I said.

'I live by them,' he replied.

He got to his feet and brushed any flecks of ash that had escaped, off his trousers.

'The car out there can get thirty-one miles to the gallon,' he said. 'I'll get a smidgen under ten gallons in the tank. I can drive to The Footlands and back without filling her up.'

In the car I sat in the back. Nothing else was said between us for a good ten minutes and then he wound down his window and said, 'You're not to mind me.'

The air was cold but refreshing, and besides I welcomed it because I was feeling drowsy due to lack of sleep. It was well past dusk. Outside the landscape was bare as far as I could see. Electricity pylons ruled the Earth, they stood out against the purple sky.

'I was told to pick up a man like you once,' he said, 'and it took me two days to drive there. I was to take him to somewhere else a further day on top of that.

'Only when I got to the room did I find out it was him, the neighbour, and he was living on his own in a shitty little bedsit.'

'So what had happened to him?' I asked.

'I don't know,' he said, 'I didn't ask. Anyway this time the whole thing passed off without incident.'

'Did X send you to pick him up?'

'Yes.'

'Do you think he knew?'

'I'm certain of it. I think he did it on purpose.'

'You think he was testing you?'

'Yes, I do.'

'And you came through with flying colours,' I said.

'I certainly did,' he said. 'I can tell you though, it was a sight for sore eyes to see the way the man had fallen,' and he honked the horn a couple of times in celebration. Then he turned on the radio, but there was only hiss and occasionally snatches of voices. He turned it off.

'It's the electricity pylons,' he said.

After a while he closed the window and I dozed with the hum of the engine and the steady whooshing of the occasional car passing on the other side of the road.

Because there were no street lamps the insides of the car seemed to close in tighter around us. I saw lights on the dash and was aware of the spill of white light somewhere in front of us, and in it, the surface of the road looked like a wall of grey water rushing down, always just ahead of us. I kept expecting to hit it head on and break through. I tried to calculate how deep it would be and how long it would take for us to make it to the other side; was it a thin even rain or an endless downpour, or were we in fact looking down on the ocean, falling vertically, yes, I was sure we were falling. I felt disoriented when I awoke and I instinctively braced myself against the back of the driver's seat. Mr Brown was whistling along to a tune that was playing on the radio. He broke off to wish me a good morning.

I looked out of the window. It was light and we were driving into a small town. I was sure we were on the outskirts; over to our left I could see industrial buildings and the odd chimney. We were slowly driving towards the town centre, I could feel it. No building on the route in was taller than a couple of floors. The roads were edged now with green verges and cherry blossom. It was early, the streets were deserted, the air was clean and the light was sharp. Even as the car moved I could see in detail the branches of the trees.

And then, just as we were about to reach what I presumed was the town centre, the houses began to thin out and the road was lined with trees all the same type and the same height.

'Where are we?' I asked.

'We're here,' he said as he pulled up outside a large red brick building. I sat forward in my seat.

'Yes,' he said, 'go in there.'

I got out of the car and he drove off. I watched until the car had reached the end of the street and turned right, finally disappearing from sight.

I felt very stiff, I had a pain in the neck and a pain in the lower back, and one of my legs had gone to sleep which made it difficult to walk, and both of my arms had ceased to move as they ought to; they just hung down at my sides, and both my hands had seized up which made it difficult to pick up my case.

Further to this I could only hear what sounded like a rushing stream in my ears and I saw little of the true view before my eyes, I could only marvel at the bright colours that washed across my vision. My head was full of cotton wool and my lungs were folded up and stuffed into the top of my shirt.

After standing there for a few minutes waiting for my limbs and my senses and the deepest organs in my body to recover, I pulled myself together for a great and final effort and I followed the signs to reception, where I was greeted by a woman who made a note of my name before picking up my case and showing me to a small room on the fourth floor.

One moment I was standing disoriented on the pavement outside and a few minutes later I was disoriented on the fourth floor. In between, while I was disoriented in the lobby, I attempted to take in my surroundings. The reception desk in front of me was dominant, it was dark solid wood; behind it only the head and shoulders of the receptionist were visible in front of the honeycomb of pigeon-holes that were used to hold keys or mail.

On the desk: a potted plant at one end and at this end, an open register. There was a map of what I presumed was the local area on the wall beside reception, the town sitting like a cancerous growth in the top left-hand corner.

There was a foldaway screen opened up in front of what I learnt later was the doorway to the bar; in front of the screen the management had placed a few potted ferns in an attempt to make the screen less visible, but of course it probably had the opposite effect.

People came and went: a woman with a pile of towels, a couple coming out of the bar.

We took the lift up to the fourth floor.

As we approached the room along the landing I saw a man standing some way off down the corridor. He looked like he had always been standing there, and it was clear he had no immediate intention of going anywhere.

She unlocked the door and led me inside. The room was empty except for a bed, a bedside table, a chest of drawers, a table and chair, and a small sink with a mirror over it. On a small shelf on the wall about a foot and a half above the table there was a phone. On the table itself there was an ashtray and a laminated A4 card.

'I'm sorry,' I said, 'I was expecting a meeting.' I wasn't expecting an empty room.

'All in good time,' she said. Her English was very good but she spoke with a guttural accent, as if she was suffering from a heavy cold.

'When you've settled in there are things, I'm sure, that need to be discussed,' she said, 'but in the meantime there are a few rules, regulations and helpful tips you should make yourself familiar with.' The woman began to recite as if she was reading from a manual; she spoke in a monosyllabic tone.

'This floor,' she said, 'is served by the lift on the left as you approach from the lobby. The lift on the right serves the floors one, three, five and so on. The showers and toilets are along the landing on this floor. The conference hall, the ballroom and the canteen and bar are on the ground floor. Breakfast is between six and eight-thirty a.m. You're free to wander around the town during the day, when there are no activities, but you must be back in before ten-thirty p.m.'

'Activities?' I asked.

'Mr Wood locks the gate at ten-thirty-five prompt.' She looked at me. She must have explained all this a thousand times. 'Mr Wood is the gatekeeper,' she said. 'If you need anything, you'll see him around and about the place.'

'Was that Mr Wood in the corridor?' I asked.

'No,' she answered.

'Who was that?' I asked.

'I didn't see anyone in the corridor. Now remember what I said,' she said.

'How will I recognise him?'

'He's not only the gatekeeper,' she said, 'he's also the caretaker.'

'Oh.'

'And the odd-job man,' she added, 'he does the plumbing and electrics.'

'I'll see him around and about the place, you said?'

'Or you can make an appointment,' she said. 'He's also the counsellor, the psychiatrist and the registered first-aider.

'If you need anything in the night,' she said, 'if you're scared of the dark or you have a sudden craving for a cheese sandwich, he's the cook, the baker and the candlestick maker.'

I couldn't get another word in after this because it all started to come out of her now in a single stream.

'He can tuck you up,' she said, 'and he can dress you down he can cosset and he can mollycoddle he can play the good cop or the bad cop he has it in him to mother to father to brother to sister and on top of that he has the maturity to be grandmother or grandfather whichever you prefer and in accordance to the needs of any given situation he can stand in for your great-uncle or great-aunt if you have no immediate family he can grant wishes and he can bring down curses he can lift a hex he can cure indigestion headaches toothache earache unexplained pains in the bowel undiagnosed pains in the arse and any general malaise with indescribable symptoms and he can also cure a hangover.'

I nodded.

'He can also give good advice and he can administer the proper and appropriate punishment he reads minds he can read indecipherable texts and he can read any situation and act accordingly and in accordance with any given situation.'

There was a fine mist of perspiration, from her efforts, on her top lip. She then began to move around the room, brushing down the bed, moving a glass from here to there, pulling the curtains to, adjusting the chair and the table.

When she had finished she stood in front of me again. There was a thick fog of sweat on her brow, from her exertions, running down into her eyebrows, and there was a puddle formed in the indent at the base of her throat.

'If you need any of these things or anything else,' she said finally, 'he's the man to look out for.'

'Yes,' I said.

The water in her shoes squelched as she walked out of the room.

When I was left alone I sat on the bed and considered the layout of the room. If my calculations were correct I was sleeping with my feet facing west, which I had heard once was a good thing (or was that if your feet were facing east?). I noticed the soap on the sink was worn to a thin sliver and this made me take a moment to consider who had been in the room before me. Otherwise the sink was clean, marked only by intractable tidemarks. The sheets were laundered and I wondered at the way the blankets had been arranged on the bed; instead of the customary tucking in on both sides and folding back over at the pillow end, these were tucked in down one edge and folded back along the length of the bed, effectively bisecting it.

I stood up and walked to the table. I picked up the laminated card. On it there was a list, which read: 'Room Service 901, Maintenance 902, Dr 903, Front Desk 904, Gen Enq 906.' Then under that it said: 'The bar on the ground floor has every kind of famous drink.'

There was a map of the fourth floor.

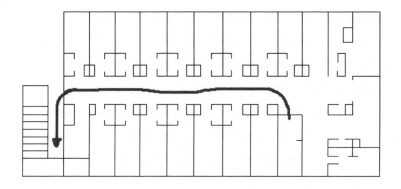

Drawn onto the map in red crayon there was a line from my room to the stairs, signifying the escape route in the event of a fire, but the line wavered slightly as if the evacuee was drunk. Under the map it read: 'In case of evacuation the lifts are not in use.' This was repeated in a number of other languages. I put the card back on the table.

There was a single window and drawn across it a chequered curtain that was attached by rings to a pole, like a shower curtain. I pulled it back and looked out. Below me there was a square and a children's playground, surrounded on every side by tall buildings with many floors.

In the square there was a man walking his dog and there was a woman walking her dog. The dogs stopped and sniffed at each other's arses but the man and the woman didn't seem to exchange any pleasantries at all.

All around the square, looking out onto the climbing frame, the roundabout, the swings and the slide, there were the remains of park benches; the skeletal frames that held the planks of wood to sit on and watch the children enjoying themselves were there, and yet the planks of wood themselves, on all of the benches, were missing.

I saw a couple in one of the windows in the building opposite. They stood facing each other. I wondered for a minute what they were saying, if they were rowing with each other, or maybe he was saying, 'I love you for ever' and she was replying,

'But I love another' and him considering how he could murder her and get away with it.

But after a while any interest I had in them dissipated into the thin air. I saw clouds gathering, and over the mountains the sky was smudged with distant rain.

I turned back into the room and thought about taking a shower. I opened the door and stepped into the corridor. I noticed first of all that it was darker than I had remembered. I took a step forward and contemplated whether I should go left or right if I wanted to go to the washroom. As I did so the lights came on. After that the first thing I saw was the man still standing in the corridor. He obviously hadn't moved because the sensors had not picked up any movement from him, which would have switched on the lights. I looked at him. He was looking at me, as if he had anticipated the exact position I would find myself standing in. Without acknowledging him I stepped back into my room and closed the door.

I stood for some time wondering what to do, because the man had unnerved me, when suddenly there was a loud knocking. I was startled, standing so close to the door as I was, and I almost cried out. (So now I was startled as well as being unnerved.) There followed a further bout of loud knocking on the door, which as a result rattled in its frame. I was afraid it wouldn't take another pounding. (Now then, I was afraid as well.)

I considered not opening it, but that wasn't really an option; after all it was clear enough that I had not gone out. For now I decided if I did nothing for long enough the problem would go away. I waited for the sound of footsteps receding but none came. (But then I had heard none arrive either.)

Finally I opened the door and the man who had been standing some way down the corridor was now standing there, right in front of me.

I looked him up and down. I could see he was thinning on top, his hair was cut short, perhaps to compensate, but this only further accentuated his deep forehead, which was lined – a mass of tiny creases and deeper furrows – both when he was at rest and when he was in the process of expressing an emotion and getting a point across. His cheeks were hollow, his lips were chapped, his eyes were wild, his eyebrows were lively, his ears were slightly protruding, his mouth was full of ravenous teeth set in three lines. I won't even begin to describe his body, which seemed at times to be short and fat and at others to be long and thin, and on the third occasions to be neither, instead seeming to exist somewhere in a state of flux, a body both fat and thin and at the same time both short and tall. He fitted in with what was required of him on every different occasion.

He wasn't wearing any shoes. He stood in his socks. That accounted for the fact that he had approached the door unheard.

'Are you Mr Wood?' I asked.

'No, my name is Walter,' he replied. And then: 'Can I come in?'

'What?' I asked.

'Can I come in?'

'Why?'

'I'm next door,' he said, as if that was qualification enough. What it did explain though, was why he was out in his stockinged feet.

'Next door?' I said.

'Yes.'

He was unflinching, but luckily so was I. We stood face to face, both waiting for the other to submit, me waiting for him to turn on his heels and scurry away, he waiting for me to stand aside and allow him entry.

Occasionally he'd glance past me into the room and I'd counter this by looking longingly into the middle-distance and licking my lips. Then he would put his right hand into his right jacket pocket as if he was about to pull something threatening out of it, but he would always withdraw his hand empty again, and every time he employed this tactic I would buff one of my shoes on the back of the other trouser leg, perhaps three strokes upward and three strokes downward.

For the next round he did the same but with his left hand and I responded, just as before, but with the other shoe on the other leg.

And soon enough we fell into sync with each other and this went on for some time, I think because a rhythm was quickly established, which in itself became a pleasant way to spend the morning.

It wasn't too long though before the whole ritual became merely habitual and there was room to allow the attention to wander. I began to think of other things, as I'm sure he did. In point of fact I'd suggest it's the ability to allow the mind to wander like this, without losing the focus, that makes one successful in this kind of stand-off situation.

But when the actions lost their meaning altogether and it became merely a war of attrition, which one of us was forced to win and one of us certain to lose, in the end he could do nothing but submit.

He said, 'Listen though, before you go, I wanted to have a quick word with you.'

I said nothing. I thought, let him come up with something.

'I saw you arrive,' he said. 'You've just arrived. I thought you might be at a bit of a loss.'

'A loss?' I said.

'It's all very new to you, I know. I wanted to say that if you have any questions…'

And then he seemed to break off.

I considered a response. No, first of all I wondered if he'd finished because his remark seemed to me to remain half-formed. But he was looking at me expectantly, and from this I was led to infer he'd said as much as he was going to say, and only then did I consider my response. I admit it would probably have been better to begin considering my response while I was waiting to see if he had finished, and then alter it according to any further additions he might make – in short, be confident enough in myself to think I could be flexible enough to assess and re-assess from second to second, from statement to statement. But I was stalled in the blocks. I presumed he was offering me assistance and advice, and to this I had to ask myself, Why should I put any of my trust in this man? I considered asking him to give me an indication of his qualifications at least – if not his CV, then perhaps a list of referees – but before I was able to formulate a reply he spoke to me again (from this I deduced that patience was not one of his virtues), he said, 'Let me pre-empt you if you don't mind.'

Oh good god, I thought.

'I can probably account for most of what has happened to you so far,' he said. 'I know you must have made it this far by using your own initiative. Am I right? But what I've got, more than the next man, is knowledge of the things you have yet to face. You see?'

He looked very happy with himself. I resolved though to continue to make things difficult for him.

'And there's no use you going and asking that woman

anything,' he said, 'because her lips are sealed. She's on the payroll you see, whereas I'm on the outside, like you. I've been on the outside like you and now I'm on the inside. And I've been here long enough to know a few things about how to get by.'

It was at this point the light went off again in the corridor, and almost indiscernibly he leaned back, or he stepped back just enough to turn the lights back on again, and without taking a breath he continued on: 'And better than that,' he said, 'I've picked up a few tips on how to make the system work to your advantage. For example,' he said, 'standing in the foyer in front of the lifts. The lift on the left serves floors two, four, six and so on, she's told you that I'm sure, and the lift on the right serves floors one, three, five, seven etc., she tells everybody that, and our floor, the fourth floor, is served by the lift on the left, am I right?'

I only looked at him.

'But the lifts are slow in coming,' he said, 'which of course you don't know yet.

'I've found it to my advantage to take the first lift that comes,' he said to me conspiratorially, 'if it's the one on the left all the better, but if it's the lift on the right, I take it, get out at five and walk down, or get out at three and walk up, depending on whether I think I need the exercise. More often than not I would get out at five.'

'Stop there,' I said. 'I have to take a shower.'

I had begun to itch.

'Perhaps we can continue this in the bar later,' I added. I was surprised to find that the barriers I had erected between us had simply fallen away the longer he had continued talking, and the incident with the light sensor had sealed it for me. Momentarily I had the feeling that I wanted to place my life in this man's hands.

'Eight o'clock,' he said. So I nodded, and I tried to give him a little smile to back it up. When I began to push the door to, he said, through the crack, 'You know of course the bar is full of spies.'

'What?' I said.

He said, 'What about my room?'

'I need a drink,' I said.

He nodded. I closed the door. I sat on the bed and had a scratch.

My loneliness had become tangible by this point. While I was at once profoundly suspicious of any new person I met, I was, at the same time, desperate for some comfort from another human being.

The moods I suffered, good followed by bad, were coming in cycles with me. One day I would prefer to be alone, but on another day I would wake in a bad mood and it would stay with me. These are the times when, if I had a friend to talk to, I might be brought out of myself.

I took the pile of postcards from my case and put them on the table in front of me. By some accident, maybe I knocked the pile over or something, I came across this picture of a coastline among the others, which were all of the wood-panelled room. This discovery seemed to lift my spirits because I saw it as a sign of better things to come.

I met Walter in the bar at eight o'clock as we had arranged; he was waiting for me, greeting me with an exaggerated smile as I approached.

We sat down with a pint and drank in silence.

On the way down I was thinking, What a solid fellow he seems to be, while I was also nervous, as if I was on a first date.

In the course of the early part of the conversation that started up he told me he had arrived here by boat. 'On the day,' he said, 'I could see very little out of the porthole except a patch of blue sky that was interrupted occasionally by the taller buildings on the shore. I couldn't get off my bunk,' he said. 'I come from a big town and had never dreamt of a life by the ocean,' he said, 'but I met a woman and it was because of her that I ended up at the seaside. We had a few days walking on the beach hand in hand. In the end I said goodbye to her on the dock as she set sail.

'Soon after that,' he said, 'I was enlisted to the service of a pleasure boat that left the pier four times a day and took a sightseeing trip around the harbour. It was my job to hand out publicity material in the Town Square.'

The landlady was leaning on the bar and looking at us, probably not out of any particular interest I thought, but simply because there was not much else to look at. She had her elbows down on the counter and her hands clasped together in front of her, and this pushed her breasts together so that her cleavage became something I was interested in for the moment. It also came to my attention that she had on a low-cut top, which had short sleeves, and you could see all of her arms as well; most of what was on show over the top of the bar was bare flesh.

Walter though had started talking again, and there was an earnestness to his tone (and I would always think this about him) that was impossible to ignore, that pinned you down and wouldn't let you get away, and it most often demanded you look at him as well, making it almost impossible to get even an occasional sly look at the landlady's cleavage, for example.

'The man who gave me the job with the pleasure cruisers,' he said, 'was called Skipper. And as well as organising the crew, he also sang in a nightclub. I saw him once.

'You see, when I was lying in the bunk later, I could hear him singing somewhere, off in the distance. He had said to me on my first day, 'Don't worry, handing out leaflets isn't going to be for ever, one day you'll be manning the lifeboats.'

'I was only living for the moment though and I didn't care what I did.'

I nodded.

'Then on this one particular trip we suddenly didn't dock as usual and we didn't turn back, we sailed out into open water. I was on my back in the staff quarters. They couldn't get me up. The blood had turned to salt in my veins.'

He paused and I did nothing to fill the silence, it hung between us, and this was perhaps the effect he was looking for, I thought later, this hanging silence between us, it was very effective, a word from me might have broken the spell. Anyway it meant he could start talking again and be certain the next words would be charged with tension.

'I maintain to this day that I was shanghaied,' he said pointedly, 'because I shouldn't have been on the boat in the first place.

'I was caught because I was sick, and I was brought here with the rest of them, and at the dock they picked us up and loaded us onto buses.'

I said, 'I also feel there are promises that have been broken,' but I couldn't properly put them into words, so I told him something about my trip and a bit about where I had come from.

'I didn't come from a place like that,' he said. 'I've been a barrow boy, a newspaper boy and the boy wonder to a caped crusader on bank holidays. I've even been a college boy,' he added, and 'a rent boy, a minor and I've worked in the steel industry.' He finished off with a flourish.

I told him the number of floors I had been in charge of. He said he'd never been in charge of a single floor and that was something he regretted to this day. He said, 'Anyway, before all that I must have been a schoolboy. I suppose that goes for all of us.'

'Yes.'

'Do you know,' he said finally, 'sitting there, you remind me of my father, as he was then, when I was a schoolboy and I knew him.' His voice sounded slightly cracked all of a sudden. 'You have the same look in your eye,' he said, 'like you might remember all the things that have passed between us, as father and son.'

'No, I don't think so,' I said to defend myself.

'Listen,' he said, 'I wonder if you wouldn't mind looking away for a moment, I feel quite emotional all of a sudden. I feel I might cry and make a fool of myself.'

I turned away and had a mouthful of beer. The woman behind

the bar was drying glasses; as she vigorously plunged the towel into and out of the open end of the glass her tits bounced up and down as if she was juggling them on her forearms.

'No, it's all right. I can never cry like that again,' he said, interrupting my reverie. 'Drink up.'

We both drank, then he said, 'Listen, what sort of thing is it we grow up into?'

'I don't know,' I said.

'When is it that the aspirations you have for me as a father become the aspirations I have for myself, the two often incongruous of course, and the moment dawning – sometimes embraced and sometimes bitterly fought – when you must hand over the reins to me and be done with it?'

I looked at him. I didn't know what to say, I thought about saying 'I don't know' again, then I thought about asking him if he was talking to me or addressing his father?

'Everything is going to be okay,' he said, 'in fact I've never felt better. That thing about my father,' he said, 'it's something that comes up every now and again, I feel I have some issues there, to sort out, but as of yet I haven't had the time to get round to it. Anyway it isn't worth getting alarmed about. Forgive me,' he said.

We looked at each other. I drained my glass. He was still looking at me.

'Do you forgive me?' he asked after some time.

'Yes,' I said, 'of course. There's nothing to forgive.'

He grinned at that.

'Another two pints over here,' he called at the woman behind the bar, raising his arm in the air and clicking his fingers. 'She won't bring them of course,' he said.

Taking my glass in one hand and his, still a quarter full, in the other, he got to his feet and went to the bar. I saw him finish his, while waiting for refills.

Apart from a man sitting alone to our right and a couple in the corner there was no one else in the room but us, apart from the woman pouring the drinks of course. I wondered if any of them were spies and whom they could be spying for.

I looked around the room; in effect it was split into two: the saloon, on this side of the dividing line, was predominantly varnished dark wood; the bar tables were dark wood, all the fixtures and fittings, the bar itself, while underfoot was a gaudily patterned carpet that at first glance appeared to be red, or crimson, in colour, but at closer inspection was a mass of closely-knit swirls and leaf-like structures. The bar sat in the dead centre of the room, like an island.

Beyond it the carpet was replaced by grey lino, the wallpaper ended and the walls were simply emulsioned a light grey; between the two a thin strip of wood held the two halves together.

The other side of the room, because it wasn't currently in use, was mostly in shadow; it all disappeared into the gloom.

At the far end I was just able to make out what was an enlarged and slightly blurred black and white photograph taking up the whole back wall, a poor reproduction of a painting, I think. It was a dark scene, or at least the photograph was dark.

On a long table, a feast was laid out: whole fruit, a pig's head with an apple in its mouth, goblets of wine, that sort of thing. There was a dwarf standing on the table at one end. He had long curly hair, probably fashionable at the time, and a beard. He was wearing a large-brimmed black hat (I presume it was black), and pantaloons. A sword in its scabbard was slung from the belt round his waist – it hung down over the edge of the table (it must have dragged on the floor behind him when he was on solid ground). He had his arm in the air, and a silver or pewter goblet in his hand.

The other people, seated the whole length of the table, looked gleefully at him, he in turn looked gleefully at the rest of the people around the table, and only the pig with the apple in its mouth didn't look gleeful; it looked glassy-eyed.

I thought, They'll be toasting the generosity of their host.

'This is also the canteen,' Walter said as he sat back down. He must have read my mind. 'You'll come in here for your breakfast tomorrow morning,' he added and he nodded into the dark maw behind the bar.

'In there?'

'Yes,' he said.

I noticed now there was a long table in front of the picture, against the back wall, and on the table were a number of empty metallic containers, piles of plates and a rack of cutlery.

I had a sip of beer. It tasted sweet.

'Listen Walter,' I said after we had been sipping our beer for a minute, 'how long do I have to stay here?'

'I don't know,' he replied.

'Well how long have you been here?' I asked.

'That I don't know either,' he said, 'not for sure anyway, I've lost track of the time. Too bloody long though,' he added and he took a sip of his beer. 'It's taking longer with me,' he said, 'because they haven't got my records.'

'How do you mean?' I asked.

'I told you I was shanghaied.'

'Yes.'

'Well, I suppose they weren't expecting me. And it doesn't help that this place is run in such an inefficient way,' he said. 'There are many people working behind the scenes so they tell me, but you won't find anybody on the shop floor.

'To be honest I think I could do a much better job of it myself,' he said. 'Somebody needs to take the whole enterprise by the scruff of the neck and shake it. All manner of crap would fall out.'

'And you're the man for the job,' I said.

He laughed and then he said, 'Do you know, sitting here talking to you has inspired me. I've been thinking I should take my suggestions to the authorities for some time now, you see I have a hundred ideas, but it's only now that I feel motivated to get off my arse and do it.

'It can't do any harm can it?' he added. 'If some of the ideas are taken on board, all the better, if not at least it will give them a chance to assess their existing procedures.'

'I suppose so,' I said.

'I shall make a note of all the things I imagine will improve the place. I could do that first thing and have a word with the people in charge tomorrow. I'm sure I can get things moving along. Maybe you could come along with me and act as my deputy.'

I must have had a startled expression on my face because he quickly went on to qualify, 'I don't mean deputy. No, I don't mean deputy. Of course you wouldn't have to do anything. I mean you would accompany me as a kind of witness, as a character referee if you like. How does that sound?'

'Well...'

'And there's no time like the present, is there?' he added.

'I'm not sure I should be stirring things up on my first day here,' I said. After a momentary silence he agreed, 'No, of course not, you're right,' he said. 'You don't even know me, do you? We've only just met. You know nothing about me. Maybe it wasn't such a good idea after all.'

'I don't mean that it isn't a good idea,' I said.

'No, it's a terrible idea,' he replied. 'You were right. I don't suppose I could do any better. What makes me think I can do any better?'

'I think the thing you said...' I muttered. 'I'm just not expecting to be staying here long,' I added, more purposefully, 'because I have a connection to make. You understand I don't want to become embroiled in any of the day-to-day business...'

We both had a mouthful of beer. It tasted sour. It must have been something to do with the lining of my mouth. My mood was both sweet and sour, while my mind drifted off somewhere else, to the landlady's cleavage, or the dwarf toasting the landlady's cleavage.

'Perhaps tomorrow we can look round the town,' I said to finally change the subject.

'Maybe,' he replied, 'I'm certainly the man who can show you everything the town has to offer.'

He seemed to be dwelling a little on his recent defeat, I thought, although he once more had the wild look in his eye. I might add I found it all rather exhilarating.

At first I suppose, while I had been sitting upstairs in my room, I had only been able to imagine myself drifting around the place in the half-light in the full light in the half-light again and then finally in the dark, maybe unable to find my way back to my bed. Now I had a trip out to look forward to.

At ten-thirty there was an announcement over the Tannoy. We all retired to our rooms.

I was standing in the hall with Walter, outside my door, when I realised that I was somewhat apprehensive about leaving him and spending the rest of the night on my own. He shook my hand and disappeared into his room. I found myself alone in the corridor for a moment. I missed him already.

I wondered if there was anyone else on our floor.

A few minutes later, lying in my bed, I noticed there was no shade on my light-bulb. I listened for the sounds of the building around me. There was the clanging of the old pipes, doors closing, muffled coughs, under my door I could see the light in the corridor blink on; I lay and waited for it to go off again. Then I noticed the tap on my basin was dripping, I hadn't heard it at first, after all I had been training my ear on the creaks in the middle- and the far distance, but now that I had tuned my ear to the few feet around my bed, it became all-consuming. I couldn't hear anything else. All sensible thoughts that had been in my head were drowned out by it. I tried to focus on the sounds in the middle- and far distance again but was unable to, so I got up and tried to turn the tap off. It was as tightly closed as it could possibly be and wouldn't budge any more.

Anyway as a result I must have slept fitfully because in the morning I struggled to get out of my bed.

After I had dressed I knocked on Walter's door, but nothing stirred inside and he didn't answer it. I wondered whether he had gone down to breakfast without me. When I got to the canteen though, he was nowhere to be seen.

I ate very little, the food was quite disgusting; the brown liquid was unrecognisable as coffee, if that's what it was supposed to be.

I was tired, the dripping tap had kept me awake most of the night.

I met Walter in the lobby as I made my way to reception to make a complaint.

'Are you mad at me?' he said immediately, before we had even had the chance to greet each other. He looked pale.

'What?' I said.

'My behaviour last night; all that stuff about my father, trying to involve you in one of my hair-brained schemes, and then not straight away promising to show you around the town when you had specifically asked me to.'

'Not at all,' I said.

'Then you're not mad at me?' he asked. 'I was up half the night worrying I'd offended you in some way, and then I overslept this morning.'

'No,' I said, 'not at all.'

'And when you didn't invite me down to breakfast, of course I feared the worst,' he said.

'I did knock,' I said, 'but there was no reply and I presumed you were up already.'

'I wasn't up,' he said. 'I overslept. I was up half the night, and now I might have missed breakfast.'

'I wasn't offended in any way,' I assured him.

'No, of course not,' he replied, 'how could I have thought such a thing? What could have put an idea like that into my head? By the way,' he said, 'how did you sleep?'

'Not very well,' I said.

'Ah,' he said knowingly. 'It's true the beds are torture machines. If I were in charge that would be something I'd change immediately. And I'd make sure you were able to have a lie-in, too. Listen, don't you worry,' Walter added, 'I shall take my complaints to the very highest authority. I won't have you sleeping on a bed like that.'

'It wasn't the bed,' I said.

'I never sleep well the first night in a strange bed either, in fact I'm convinced it's a common grievance,' he said. 'Maybe we should give the bed another night or two, to see how it stands up, before we lodge a complaint about it.'

'It wasn't the bed,' I said again, 'it was the tap in my room that was dripping.'

'Ah,' he said, 'the plumbing in this place is shot to shit.'

That was seemingly the natural end to the conversation. Walter stood for a moment and then he looked at his watch.

'This Mr Wood,' I said to him, 'have you seen him about the place by any chance?'

'No,' he said, somewhat downcast. 'No, I haven't.'

'I was just on my way to reception,' I said.

'Yes, that's probably the best thing to do,' he said. 'I'm going to see about a bit of breakfast.' With that he disappeared into the canteen.

The woman on the reception desk didn't know anything about Mr Wood either.

'That department has got nothing to do with me,' she said.

'The woman who showed me to my room said I'd see him around and about the place.'

'We all have our own arrangements,' she replied. 'What was the name of this woman?' she asked because I hadn't gone away. 'It's possible that she has some kind of arrangement that I don't know about.'

'I don't know,' I said.

'What did she look like?' she asked. 'It may be that she has something organised that I haven't been informed of.'

'She was middle-aged,' I said.

'Hold on a moment,' she said.

I could tell she was irritated with me and would prefer it if I went away and left her alone. She got up and disappeared into the room behind the reception desk.

There then followed a sort of stand-off between us.

First of all I stood there for a long time, before I saw her glancing to see if I had moved on. I saw her eye at the crack of the door, and as soon as I saw this I tried to assume an expression of contentment, as if I was happier than I had ever been, standing there waiting for her.

This went on for some time, her glancing through the crack to see if I had moved on, me assuming an air of contentment at being there, with misty eyes and lips upturned slightly at the corners. Because I considered this one of my talents, these silent stand-offs, I knew in the end she would have to relent. Finally, as I knew she would, she did. She returned to her post and acted as if she had only been away for a minute.

'I'm afraid she isn't in at the moment,' she said. 'You'll need to try again later. Or tomorrow would be better still,' she added.

'Tomorrow?' I said.

'Tomorrow would be better,' she said, 'but you can try again later if you like.'

'I'll try again later,' I said.

I went immediately up in the lift to my room. I thought about the tap and tried to disassemble it there and then, and see if I could work out the problem, but I needed tools, I needed a spanner to loosen the nut, and I needed a washer; it was probably a petrified washer that was the problem.

I picked up the telephone handset to dial for Maintenance. Why hadn't I thought of that before? There was no dialling tone though, there was only the sound of a great emptiness, as if the handset had been picked up simultaneously somewhere else in the deepest darkest part of the building and was being held to an unknown ear. I pictured the unknown face to go with it, its mouth slightly open, the breath that must have been in it, held, so that no sound was forthcoming. I was made uneasy by this and replaced the receiver immediately.

Later Walter said, 'Don't worry, I'm making a note of this, it's very useful for somebody like me to have somebody like you giving fresh insights on ways the whole set-up can be improved. Anyway,' he added, 'why don't we have a go at fixing the tap ourselves? I'll take you into town and we can buy the necessary tools.' I agreed. But every day we failed to make it into town: on my second day we both took a nap in the afternoon; I was exhausted and even the tap couldn't keep me awake; it turned out that both of us had only closed our eyes for a moment, each relying on the other to knock on the door, so we slept through until dinner-time.

The next day, Walter said he couldn't take me into town because he had to compose his great manifesto. 'You see, I've decided to submit my plans for the reorganisation of this place to the highest authority after all,' he said, 'and I can't go in there unprepared, they're likely to try and pick holes in anything I suggest. But don't worry, I'll definitely take you into town tomorrow,' he said.

When the next day came he said, 'I can't take you into town today because my great manifesto is taking me longer to compose than I thought it would. When I sat down last night with a piece of white paper in front of me, and determined to fill it immediately with my superior ideas and intentions, I had a few problems with a particular clause, you see I couldn't quite fix it properly into words,' he said, 'but I shall certainly take you into town tomorrow, if the weather holds out.'

He shut himself up in his room for days on end to write the manifesto and of course we never made it into town.

Meanwhile I had gone back to the front desk to follow up my complaint. It was a different woman at the reception desk, even though it was the same complaint. Would I like to fill out another form about the faulty tap and post it in my box? she wanted to know. I didn't know anything about any boxes or any forms, I told her.

I learnt that when I'd complained about the tap a report should have been filed that would have gone off to the person dealing directly with my case, to which I must have looked crestfallen, because she asked me while I was at it if I would like to make a complaint against the receptionist who was on duty and didn't post the form? I told her I didn't, and I decided not to complain about the tap either, because I figured if I was in contact with the person dealing directly with my claim through this arrangement with the pigeon-holes, which I understood to be unsatisfactory, I thought it would better serve me to make some enquiries about my forthcoming meeting with X. This way, I decided, I was forced to get out of here in time to meet my connection. So I filled in the form with renewed hope, requesting that my interview be organised quickly, because I had a flight to catch.

Walter's grand ideas about reorganising the place quickly became more revolutionary in nature. At first he had an idea that constructive criticism might be the answer, but this was soon replaced by more radical schemes.

One day he said to me, 'The most important thing now is to recruit a few like-minded individuals to the cause. I already have another body on board. His case is in the same sorry state as mine, and he's happy to see what he can do to help. You must meet him,' he added. 'From what I know about him and what I have learnt about you, you'll get on like a house on fire.'

I told him I was happy to meet him, but as far as involving myself in his plans for the overthrow of the existing order, I had other things playing on my mind.

I went back to reception every morning to see what, if anything, had happened with regard to my written enquiry. For the first few days my form was still there, sticking out of the pigeon-hole, and it took a few more fruitless days before my box was finally emptied, which was a start, but every day after that it remained empty of course, until, after a week or so had gone by and nothing had happened, I decided to make a complaint.

I stood in front of the receptionist and wrote down what I had to write. I began by saying I had already written in regard to my claim and had since heard nothing, etc., and what was to be done, etc. I said I was furious. I decided to take a bolshy tone because at the moment I clearly held the moral high ground. It was my understanding, I said, that while my case was outstanding it was the duty of the authorities to make sure that it was looked at with the most immediate effect. I always wanted to go on the offensive because I found it the best way to elicit a quick response.

Not so in this case. I had no word back, no word at all. This went on, I wrote letter after letter, one vociferous complaint following the last, until weeks and weeks had slipped by.

Walter was not surprised of course by this turn of events and promised to add the details to his report. He proposed to update them on a daily basis as the proceedings unfurled.

As for the dripping tap, I never bothered to talk about it again. In fact I came to see many things in the drip; as I lay in the dark I imagined the drop that formed and began to expand, a mirror to all that was going on around it, holding something new from every different angle it was looked at from; and then I pictured its descent and its destruction in the porcelain bowl below; every new thought that was formed, that became bloated and was broken into a thousand pieces. And I fell asleep under a thin rain.

When I woke up the next day, the sun came out for good, clearly there was no more chance of rain. It was the early morning spring light, I decided, that had woken me early, because I always slept with the curtains open; it was only when the cleaners had been in that the curtains were drawn – why did they draw the curtains? I wondered. Did they consider their tasks clandestine? I should think not. At all other times they were open.

I should have seen this coming anyway, I thought, after all, the heating had been turned off the day before, as if spring had been predicted, and here it was now, and only a day late.

Consequently the building became suddenly and surprisingly quiet. With hindsight it was obvious that it was the boilers that were noisy, but only to a level that was below the pitch that irritated the human ear; personally I found the new silence more difficult to get used to.

I lay in the bed for a few minutes and contemplated another

day in pursuit of my claim. So far I had written many letters, most of them using the same belligerent tone, and I had not had a single response. I considered a change of plan.

The spring had brought with it a breath of air from another continent (they tell me it comes from somewhere), and it had reinvigorated my desire to rise to the challenge that was put in front of me. If the bellicose tone wasn't going to work, and it clearly wasn't, I decided to change tack.

I walked over to the window; I always created my best plans and subsequent changes of plan at the window, where the vista offered the chance of change: a tree might come into bloom or begin to lose its leaves; today a child, that wasn't there the day before, might be on the roundabout; the sky was always a new shade of blue.

What could I see today? I started close-in: two men were replacing the wooden slats on the benches around the play-ground below my window. The job was nearly done. Their truck was parked on the road to one side, and it was full of planks, as if it was carrying enough park benches to serve the whole town.

As I continued to watch them, the laundry van pulled up.

Our sheets were taken away once a week; I expected the whole manoeuvre would be kicking off any minute, as usual: the stripping down of beds. Pity the poor bastards on the first floor, I always thought. They greeted the van even as I said this:

a team choreographed by habit; two of them lifted the baskets from the back of the truck, two more wheeled them out of my sight into the foyer.

Everything else we needed was also provided for us at the same time: one roll of toilet paper a week, soap, towels – they took away all the towels, even if one of them hadn't been used.

Anyway I decided to cast my view a little bit further today. I started by fixing my gaze on the building opposite. I saw the man in the window. I had rarely seen him and the woman at the same time since that first day; he had grown a moustache, or it was a different man. He moved from one side of the flat to the other, appearing first in the window on the left as I was looking at it, and then, after disappearing momentarily, he appeared in the window on the right seconds later, and he never changed this routine, he never paused, and I could say this with some certainty because I often continued his walk in my mind for the length of time he was out of sight and, looking back, I established that he never once paused or walked slower or speeded up.

As I had grown used to the view from my window over the months, I was able to see further and further afield. When I first moved in I was only able to make out the lowest foothills of the mountains on the edge of the town, but now I could see way beyond them, to the wine-growing regions, and after that to the sea, the white crests on the waves on the sea, and then the deeper deeps that were bluer and further out, and at the end of that the uncertain horizon, the sky that met it like a frayed cloth; and where it had started to come away I could see under it and it was just blackness and empty and that was as far as I was able to see today.

Everything was more crystal clear then, in the new spring light that bathed over everything, and that accounted as well for my newly improved sight, I supposed; and then I thought: all my senses are working to their best. I am in great shape. A wash, I thought, and I'll be invincible.

Between six a.m. and seven-thirty, and also in the evenings between four-thirty and six-thirty, there was hot water available in the rooms. I ran some into the sink. When the laundry came the cleaners came with it and it was better to be out of the room altogether, I found. So on this day, every week, I didn't take my shower as usual and return to my room after; I had a quick wash in the sink and went and sat in the day room.

The day room was a great hall situated on the ground floor and, being at the back of the building, it allowed the sunshine to come in during the early part of the morning. Thick, red velvet curtains dropped the whole distance from ceiling to floor across two walls, and a belt of worn carpet surrounded the polished wooden dance floor on three sides, as did thirty or forty mismatched tables, each with three or four mismatched chairs around them. Across one end of the dance floor there was a small stage with three or four steps up to it on either side. At the back of the stage, against a curtain of sparkling streamers, stood an upright piano.

During the day the residents would gather in the hall and it was an unsaid law that every resident or guest claimed their own chair. I would occasionally sit and watch as squabbles broke out over ownership of this or that seat.

Today I had another complaints form to fill in. I had long since given up completing them as I stood at the reception desk; now I took the form away and allowed myself the luxury of properly venting my spleen. Some of my diatribes stretched to thirty tightly written sides.

Today though, I thought, it's going to be different. I sat back and tried to assess what state of mind I was in and how I would translate that into words and put it down on the form.

In fact the forms had become something of a diary for me. I was certainly writing down most of my thoughts. Truthfully I had begun to lose track of their purpose and I no longer formed a picture of the recipient receiving them. This allowed me the freedom to use them to form ideas, some sketchily, and they were often dispatched with crossings-out all over them and sentences underlined or ringed for emphasis.

I met Walter in the day room. He didn't want to lock himself in his room all the time either, he said. Today he planned to become more expansive, 'but I have a lot of things on my mind,' he said he wanted to make that clear. He also told me he had a friend he wanted to introduce me to.

'Mr D,' I said.

'How do you know about him?' he asked.

'Because you talk about him constantly,' I said.

'Do I?'

'Yes.'

'Well...' he said. He suggested Mr D would have wanted to meet on neutral ground.

'Why?' I asked.

Walter sat facing me, I had my back to the door, and he was too busy bobbing up and down, looking over my shoulder to watch when somebody else came into the room, to pay me any heed.

'Who is this Mr D anyhow?' I asked.

'To be honest with you,' said Walter, 'I hardly know him.'

But Mr D didn't turn up for a long time before I said, 'What time did you arrange to meet him?' and Walter said nothing had been arranged, not a specific time anyhow. And then he still didn't turn up for ages after this little exchange. 'So listen,' I said finally, 'I've been following your advice, I mean about complaining, but it isn't coming up with anything. I have another form here I've got to fill in.' But Walter had a one-track mind, and if he was thinking about Mr D he wasn't thinking about anything else.

I was soon bored of it. For all I knew this Mr D had no intention of meeting me. Actually, he might not even exist.

'Let's go for a walk,' I said and I got to my feet, which I immediately regretted, because Walter was not in a position to get to his feet, and would clearly not be in such a position for some time yet. But I was already on my feet, and yet I didn't feel free to leave without him. It wasn't in my character to sit back down once I had gotten up either; I always wanted to plunge on ahead. So I found myself in this situation instead: I mean that I had left behind where I was and was still far from where I was intending to go to. And while I was there, this refrain kept coming into my head: Life exists in the time when you are neither incoming nor outgoing. Ha!

It turned out that Mr D didn't go for the idea of neutral ground at all and preferred that we meet him in his room.

'Come with me,' Walter said. 'Tomorrow,' I replied.

When I was alone again I tried to relocate the 'middle' ground between coming in and going out that I have just described, but was unable to, probably because the rest of the world refused to be quiet; I was exiled from it because I was unable to find it again among all the noises of spring that were in full voice: birds sang incessantly, the roads were full of a population that was stirring after the winter's hibernation, and they were all out in their cars. The people in here seemed to wake up, too: the corridors were more crowded; the walls of my room seemed to be alive with the faint sounds of conversation coming from every direction; windows around the place were left open that had previously been locked shut. I even thought I could hear the groan of the bricks moving as the building leant towards the sun.

And at night it wasn't any quieter either: the building was busy sitting back on its haunches, and inside it, within its hundred organs, nothing was silent; the water in the tanks all over the building followed the waxing and waning of the moon, lapping up against the sides of the vessels that held them in, and the floors were like a hundred diaphragms, moving up and down. Everything was alive and I was sensitive to it all.

So on my complaints form I made mention of the fact that there was nothing worse than living in a limbo like this. I said: I do not like travelling very much but this inertia is worse. I dispensed with my bolshy tone and took up this new pathetic one: Poor me, I am nothing better than a prisoner, I said. I stressed as well that I had done nothing to jeopardise my track record, I had followed out all my instructions to the letter, and if I had made errors it was certainly not through a desire to buck against the system.

I am innocent, I said.

One day soon after, and totally out of the blue, I was taken to another room and told to sit down, which I did. My seat faced a long table with chairs behind it. Four people came in and sat on the chairs, facing me: two women and two men, they sat girl boy girl boy, from the left to my right, and they introduced themselves in that order. The woman third from the left seemed to be the spokesperson; she was the only one with good English, I learnt soon enough.

At this point I'd like to take a moment out to qualify something. Not only was I surprised that something actually seemed to be happening at last, but I was also surprised to find myself unsettled by this new turn of events because I had supposed all along that I'd been hoping for this.

What had been happening to my feelings over the intervening months – between my initial desire to get out of here at all costs – and now?

It had become habitual for me to write regular letters of complaint about the lack of movement with my claim, but I also found some comfort in knowing that while nothing seemed to be moving along, I had at least been placing my thoughts on record. I questioned if that wasn't enough in itself.

I wondered also, not out loud, what had been made of my correspondence. It wasn't mentioned. The subject of my situation, however, and how it was to be approached, was quickly broached.

'Let's get straight down to business,' the spokeswoman said. And when the panel nodded in agreement, so did I.

'It's crystal clear that you haven't pursued with enough vigour the nature of your claim,' she continued. 'You see, a routine inspection has brought to light your missed connection.'

Silence. This was the situation, you see, that I had feared all along, it had been hanging over me since that first moment at the counter, when I was buying the tickets. I had missed my bloody connection. In fact it had expired, I was told in no uncertain terms, and then I was asked what I had to say in my defence.

'It hasn't been made clear to me who I am supposed to be dealing with,' I said. 'I happened across a complaints procedure quite by accident,' I added, 'and I still haven't been able to communicate directly with the officer dealing with my case.'

The other woman on the panel pushed her chair back at this point, as if she was about to leave the meeting in a huff, but instead of getting to her feet, she sat there poised on the edge of her seat. The man to the spokeswoman's left, who had a very sour face, pushed his chair back too, as if in response, until he was sitting side by side with the second woman again – but this was now a few feet behind the initial frontline – and then he suddenly got to his feet and walked out of the room. He had his forefinger in the air and his mouth slightly opened as if he had had a startling notion, a revelation, and now he was stuck in that Eureka! moment – and he held it long enough, this pose struck, until he was out of the room, where I imagined he was doused with cold water to undo it.

The second woman watched him go, with a despairing expression on her face, as if her heart was breaking, as if this might in fact be a defining moment in her life, before she rested her elbows on the table and put her head in her hands.

I took a moment here, while this drama was going on, to catch my breath and take a proper look at the room around me: the walls were off-white in colour and the carpet was grey. The table was probably false mahogany (they can make anything look like real wood these days) and there was a carafe of water on one end and four empty glasses; the water in the carafe had already begun to look cloudy.

I noticed too, at the last minute, that there was a small window high up on the wall. I could see little through it except for the clear blue of the sky, but still I began to imagine the town that lay, I thought, to the south of here: people coming and going with not a care in the world between them. If I placed my chair on the table and stood on it I would be able to gaze through the window onto what was out there: beyond the perimeter wall, fields, and then the first collections of bricks stacked into houses and around each of them low fences erected around clipped lawns, and on the other side of the fences unkempt grass, not belonging to them.

Occasionally a bird passed across the square of blue sky, which served to distract me a little from the meeting so that I never felt on top of things.

It was soon enough brought to light that I had not been properly briefed, and so subsequently it was decided that not all the blame for me missing my connection lay with me. Whom the rest of the blame lay with though, was never established.

The meeting was well and truly back into its full swing again.

'It seems to me,' the spokeswoman said, 'that you might be lacking an inquisitive nature. You must make yourself available to experience.'

'What does that mean?' I asked.

'Take some risks,' the second woman said, biting through the thickness of her heavy accent.

'You might be better served if you looked to impress yourself upon a situation rather than have the situation pressed upon you,' the spokeswoman said.

'Yes, I can see that,' I said.

'Can you?' she asked me.

'Not really.'

I had made every effort I was capable of. I was cowed though by the panel; the man who remained sat and took notes throughout, or I presumed he took notes. He might have been doodling. I have already said the second woman was prone to holding her head in her hands in mock despair, which she might have thought was harmless but was, I knew, an attempt to elicit sympathy, but she got none of it from me; I only felt sorry for myself.

It was decided anyway that I would set off immediately, or rather, that efforts would be made to make sure my connection was re-booked and all the parties concerned notified in regard to the change of timings; otherwise, the original plan was to remain unchanged in every way.

I must admit I was at a complete loss as to what was expected of me. I had been given a number of directions which I was duly expected to follow, and which I had followed, duly. How could I be responsible for any part of the plan that had gone amiss? I knew that I wouldn't get any answers here.

'I suppose you'll inform me when there's been any progress made?' I enquired.

I was assured I would be kept fully abreast of the situation.

After that the whole thing quickly petered out.

At the next meeting, which came about soon after the first, I was better prepared: the first time I had been taken by surprise and on top of that was brought to a room I had never been in; now I was familiar with the panel and the room held no surprises for me either (in fact I was able almost to shut the room out of my mind completely).

So I went on the offensive from the off and asked about the state of the plan, the original plan. I was told it had been put to one side for the moment and it had been decided, in my absence, that the new idea was that some kind of contingency plan was to be set in motion, and this even though I had thought the plan, the original plan, was going to remain unchanged (over and above the fact that the connection had to be re-booked and the interested parties notified), indeed I had been told it was to stay the same, I certainly had been.

But time can change everything, I was told, and in the unlikely event – bearing in mind the amount of time that has passed – of the original plan having become unworkable, a further plan must at least be tabled, and when it has been tabled it must be discussed until all the parties concerned are satisfied.

Finally I was assured that, although the situation appeared to be completely lost, it most certainly was not.

As for the fact that I had been unable to speak directly with the person dealing with my case, I was fobbed off with some excuse, in fact when it was explained to me it came to me as a sudden revelation, and it went something like this: apparently only one of my letters had been received by the person dealing directly with my claim! The reason for this, I was told, was that only the first letter I sent referred directly to my outstanding case, and this letter would have been given the proper and due attention accorded to it and would have been passed on immediately to the officer directly dealing with my claim.

But it would have been placed underneath a similar request for clarification by another client, and I say underneath because this other client had probably followed up this initial enquiry with a second letter and so on, a third and fourth and so on, and with the arrival of a second letter the first would invariably become more urgent and would make it to the top of the pile.

My numerous other letters, I was told – and this is where my letters were different from those of the client whose letter had reached the top of the pile before mine – were probably not letters directly referring to my initial enquiry but were most likely complaints – and I was invited almost, by the tone of their accusations – accusations? – to deny this. I couldn't of course. Were they complaints about having received no reply to my first letter? I was asked directly.

Yes.

So, although they might make mention of my case, these subsequent letters of complaint, it was probably only in passing then.

Yes.

This meant my second letter would not have been received by the person dealing directly with my claim at all, but by another officer dealing specifically with complaints about other members of staff.

And it was further posited that the third letter probably didn't mention the case at all. So every subsequent letter to that would have been received by another member of staff dealing with complaints; a complaint against the person dealing directly with my claim, a complaint against the person looking into the first complaint and so on, until it got to the very top, and then it would have been delegated to under-officers, whose job was to sift through the available documentation and follow the line of complaints back to the source. These under-officers though, for one reason or another – they might be part-time or silly in the head, and also they didn't have the same kind of access to information as those that would have been dealing with my case on the way up – might take months to make any sense of the paper trail.

This was all hypothetical guesswork on the part of the panel I might add at this point, and was offered only as a possible explanation, based on their many years of working on cases like mine.

And this is how my claim was going to get lost, I decided, amid a host of clauses and sub-clauses in respect of a hypo-thetical plan b; already I could see the negotiations were going to be nothing if not protracted and I knew then that my case would never be any closer to resolution.

I said as much in my subsequent letters of complaint. Was there no way, I wondered, to get the whole thing back on track? I was anxious that by the invention of this new plan b I was now sidetracked down a blind alley from which I feared I would never emerge again. Could I be offered some sort of guarantee that this was not to be my fate?

Further to my concerns along these lines, I added that I was willing to accept some responsibility for missing my connection. I realised that I had not been forthright enough, but it was important that we put that behind us and pressed on.

Please, I wrote, *if there is anything you can do*

Reading this back to myself I saw that I had as good as submitted, when I had actually wanted to end on a note of defiance. So I concluded by saying that I had been made aware there were other means of bringing about some satisfactory resolution to my case. I wrote, *There is a whole other world out there, running parallel to this world, an underground world, and now it is opening up to me. What am I talking about? You may well ask. The question is: should I take the matter into my own hands?*

I left it at that, an empty threat, but one that I hoped would elicit a response of some sort.

It was around this time that Walter and I suddenly had the glad eye for a woman called Colubrine and everything changed irrevocably.

From that point on I lived my days, such as they had become, hoping that I would catch a glance of her, even a very brief one:

an ankle as she disappeared around a corner ahead of me would have been enough.

She wasn't on our landing, but there were occasions when she would be seen, fleetingly, like a ghost, and then just as quickly she would disappear again. Walter and I spent a lot of our time chasing her, or what we thought was her, through the maze of corridors.

She didn't want to have anything much to do with either of us though, and it all turned out badly in the end because the whole affair drove a wedge between Walter and me. It affected his confidence badly; in many ways previous to this he had seemed unbreakable. It forced us to tell each other lies, and that was mainly how our relationship was damaged.

He started to respond to my questions with a cursory 'uh-huh'. Of course it was only another way of punishing me; he didn't want the woman, but he was angry that I had shown so much interest in her myself.

I am getting ahead of myself.

From the very beginning of my time here I had been determined not to make any attachments to this place because I was certain I would be out of it in a couple of weeks at the most. But as the weeks went by it was impossible not to find myself drawn into the life of the building as it went on around me.

The first time I saw her she was putting up bunting in the day room, I was taken with her beauty from the off; she was up a set of steps and her pneumatic thighs held the ladder in a vice-like grip as if it was only the muscles in her legs that were keeping the whole thing upright. I would have footed the ladder but someone else had beaten me to it, and I suppose I could have stood in the queue of people waiting to foot the ladder but my services were required elsewhere, pinning up signage.

The whole day I watched her though, ascending and descending into the clouds – balls of cotton that someone had strung up from the ceiling as part of the decorations.

My interest in Colubrine couldn't have come at a much worse time for Walter. His plans, he kept telling me, were moving forward at pace and he was intent on me being a pivotal part in their application, even though I was constantly distancing myself from them.

With the onset of spring we had all been put into service preparing the building for an upcoming convention of incoming men. A rota was pinned up on a notice board in the foyer and everyone was expected to pitch in: making signs, putting the signs up, putting up other paraphernalia that related to the programme of planned events etc. This only caused unrest among the residents, because it was the general consensus that the place was full enough already. Walter sensed this unease anyhow and was determined to make the most of it, while at the same time he was also convinced it was the convention that was stopping any other progress being made around the place, especially in regard to all the hundreds of cases that were outstanding, and that included mine. He said they were so bogged down with preparations that they didn't have time to knock a few more off the waiting lists.

So his attitude proved to be the populist one. He had either tapped into the public resentment or he was leading the mood himself, but whichever whatever, he was convinced a small army could be drummed up. Colubrine he considered to be a distraction from this.

As part of his recruitment drive he took me to meet Mr D in his room on the seventh floor.

Mr D let us in.

Walter knocked and we waited a full minute before the door opened, and there he was in the doorway: broad of beam and devoid of expression at first, and hugging the door frame and then the walls as I was to see was his habit, and breathing – his shirt between the buttons on his chest opening slightly and then closing again, like an artificial lung or a talking vagina more likely, to expose the pink underneath and the odd hair, and underneath that, I don't know, we were led to believe his beating heart I suppose. I only describe this in such detail because one was always aware of Mr D's breathing – all the air in every room he was in seemed to vibrate around him, waiting to be sucked in or blown out. How else can I describe it? In the end I became used to it, it was like a climate change when you went into a room that he was in.

Anyway, beyond that I'm sure I liked him, enough at least, on that first impression, to warrant a description: bug eyes, bug ears, gaping nostrils with the hairs hanging down and waving in the upward draught of air, and three chins which he wore, one during the week and the other at weekends: the third he saved for best. And then no neck to speak of – at the top it merged too quickly with his chin at the front and with the base of his skull at the back, and at the bottom it was more shoulders than it was neck. And that's just a brief sketch of the head.

Below that his body hung down – no, it didn't hang – but it definitely started from the top and worked its way down rather than beginning at the bottom and working up. And his hands, good god! He had lovely fine hands, and lovely forearms, not hairless, but not what you would call hairy either, the hairs necessary of a closer inspection I would say.

What else about him? He had a fine head of hair. He had a good set of teeth. He had a full set of fabulous buttons down the front of his jacket.

What else about him? I immediately warmed to his personality, he had personality coming out of his ears; he was chock-full of personality.

What else? Oh good god the smell of him, the luxurious

smell of him: the hair products to keep the fine head of hair in some sort of order, to prevent it getting out of hand and becoming unruly; the skin products to moisten the skin and stop it puckering at the edge of the mouth and at the side of the eyes and under the chin and at the collar of the shirt; the talcum powder no doubt spread generously in the gusset of the pant to stop sweating and chafing; and the deodorant to stop unseemly patches appearing under the arms.

What else can I tell you about him? What a magnificent specimen he was.

'Hello', he said. And on top of all that, I thought, a deep and resonant voice to go with it. Good god, I thought, listen to that voice, that voice puts the cherry on the top. What a package.

I only nodded as he showed us in, I couldn't speak, I only nodded, and shallowly, so that I didn't have to take my eyes off him. I was speechless up to this moment, and I am still speechless now, a moment after, but suddenly it's for different reasons, because as quickly as he made such a fine impression on me, he was already beginning to fade in my estimation. Yes, as far as I was concerned he wasn't so much a glorious specimen as just a man. Perhaps I have been a little premature, I thought. As quickly as I had initially become infatuated with him I soon began to see some of his negative points and they immediately began to niggle at me: for a start he had the terrible habit of looking me in the eye, and when he did his eyelids began to flicker and his pupils exploded into the sharp surrounding blue of his irises like ink released in a puddle of water. It gave the disconcerting impression of a man suddenly passing over to the other side, and however much the lines round the eyes might desperately attempt to convey feelings and emotions, the blacker the eye the deader the soul inside appears to the outside world.

What else?

He was obviously the latest in a long line of brutes, I was sure of it.

What else?

I hold my hands up and say if he was bad he might just as easily be good, and I said to myself I could be convinced with a decisive argument either way. He was though, at the end of the day, the last bastard at the end of a line of tireless bastards and he was a slippery fucker, and I was determined I would not allow myself to be silenced by him. So I looked for an opportunity to speak. But unfortunately he had stalled, and the silence that was the result of him stalling was like a sock being stuffed in my mouth.

The most disturbing thing about all this for me I suppose was that I couldn't get away from the feeling he had manipulated the whole thing: he was charming to begin with, that's true, but when Walter was distracted he cast a glance at me and turned my whole first impression of him on its head. And looking back, I think that might have been his intention from the start.

What could be the meaning behind that, I wondered.

He had spent a lot of his time turning his room into a bloody palace. We took our shoes off and put them in a wicker basket to one side of the door, and we sat on a Chesterfield sofa that was so large I wondered how the removal men had got it into the room without sawing the legs off it. Walter admired the shag-pile rug while I sat in silence and waited for the tea Mr D was brewing up.

Finally Walter said: 'What about the wallpaper in here, eh?'

'Yes,' I said. It was flock. The fourth wall was painted a different colour, which meant it became the focus of the room, and hanging on it was a large oval mirror in which I saw him fussing over the teapot (until I moved my head to the side and lost sight of him).

All the lighting in the room came from the two standing lamps and a small reading lamp that sat on an occasional table by the reclining chair facing us across the smoked glass coffee table. The book Mr D had just put down lay opened and face down by a glass of red wine.

In the corner of the room, on top of a glass cabinet, which contained hundreds of ornamental animals of all descriptions, sat a silver cup that Mr D had obviously won as a youngster, in some sporting competition no doubt; it held pride of place, and flanking it on the left and right were pictures of what I presumed were his family.

There were numerous other pictures on the walls too, of animals in their natural environments: a lion in the long grass, an elephant at the watering hole, and another picture that particularly grabbed my attention; it looked like it had been painted by a child, and it featured two sea eagles swooping down on what was obviously supposed to be a duck but looked more like a flying beagle, a duck's body with the head of a dog. But the main thing about it was that the dog/duck hybrid was desperately trying to get away with its life.

After the introductions were over Walter said to me, 'First of all I wanted to bring you up to speed.

'While you have been distracted by matters of love,' he continued, addressing me, 'our plans have been moving along nicely.'

'What have you got in mind?' I asked.

'Something more proactive,' he said. 'I don't know yet. I was hoping between us we could come up with something.

'Perhaps a small explosion,' he added after a moment's thought.

'Don't be ridiculous,' I said.

'But there's no better time,' he said, 'what with this convention coming up. We could cause mayhem.'

I told him I didn't think desperate measures like this were called for just yet.

'Anyway it doesn't matter what you think,' he said, 'because I don't need you. I've already got Mr D onside.'

'Have you?'

'Mr D is up for it, aren't you Mr D?'

'Sure,' said Mr D.

'What about the manifesto?' I asked.

'I've decided the manifesto is not the best way to approach the problem.'

'How do you mean?'

'Well I had to scrap what I'd written,' he said. 'I threw the whole bloody thing away. The tone of it was completely wrong. I had problems with the opening paragraph, which I was never able to resolve. I was banging my head against a brick wall. And then I realised: the main thing I've been having problems with is that decisions are being made somewhere above me in the chain and I don't know how high up it goes. That's the problem,' he said, 'I don't know fully whom I'm supposed to be addressing myself to. It's like my hands have been tied behind my back,' he added.

'I can't believe you're talking about planting a bomb,' I said.

'I just want you to know we are radicalised,' he said. 'It was Mr D's idea.'

Mr D looked at me again, and with this look I was unsure what I was supposed to feel; in fact my mind went completely blank.

'I like him,' Walter said to me in the bar, where we went as soon as we'd left him. 'I think he'll be an asset.'

Walter was talking to me again as if I was part of his madcap plans. It was proving useless me telling him I didn't want anything to do with them. I looked elsewhere for a spanner I might throw in the works.

'I thought so too,' I said, 'but then I saw that look in his eye.'

He lowered his beer glass slowly.

'What look?' he asked.

'It was a gleaming.'

'A gleaming?'

'Yes.'

'You thought about this after?' he asked. 'You thought you might have liked him,' he said, 'and then remembering the gleam you reconsidered?'

'Yes.'

'And you thought of all the things this gleam could mean I suppose, in your own opinion?'

'I did,' I said.

'So what did you come up with?'

'I thought maybe he was busy thinking about something else when he didn't think I was paying him any attention,' I said, 'and at the very moment I looked at him, he turned to look at me, and it was then I saw the gleam, and he saw that I had seen the gleam and perhaps also the removal of the gleam, which of course he would have set into action instantaneously and without conscious thought quick as a flash, but certainly not quick enough to prevent me seeing his true nature.'

'What?'

'I mean in the moment after a gleam is wiped off the face, the face is left blank in anticipation of the next feeling, and in that moment the true personality shows through.'

'Don't be so bloody stupid,' Walter said.

If Mr D had been working some kind of magic trick on me, I told myself, at least I had managed to escape from it. Looking back on it now, I would also say: don't be so sure.

We ordered pint after pint. I returned again and again to buy more drinks so that I could look at the landlady's cleavage, which today was a perfectly shaped v. I whispered, causing her to lean over the counter to hear me. I could see she was wearing a lacy bra. She knew, of course, exactly what I was up to.

At some point Colubrine arrived and immediately was engulfed by a pack of ravenous men in front of the bar. For a moment I forgot the barmaid's cleavage and looked on Colubrine's magnificent flanks; I was convinced that every part of her was moving, even when she was standing still.

At this time she was probably unaware of my interest, after

all I had only looked at her so far from a safe distance.

Walter suddenly stood on his chair and announced to the whole room that soon he would be running things, and the drinks would be on the house.

I brought back the pints.

Walter looked into the yellow liquid as if he was going to drown in it and then he took a sip. I went off to pee.

At the urinal I held my cock in my hand and felt the thick stream vibrating against my fingers as it travelled down the length of it. I shook off the last drops too vigorously so that it started to fill up with blood. At the same time my head was beginning to spin with the alcohol.

When I returned to the bar, Colubrine was sitting at our table with Walter. For a moment I didn't think I would be able to make the last few steps back to my chair.

As I approached, I heard Walter ask her, 'Would you like a drink?' He placed his hand on my stomach to prevent me passing and taking my seat.

'I have one,' she replied, holding up her glass.

And so, relieved of any duties, I was allowed to sit down next to her.

I knew that I probably loved her and I immediately wondered how I could make her love me. I could see she was full of aspirations and good intentions, I could see many secret things about her already, so we were obviously made for each other, but I didn't know yet whether she would be able to see all that for herself, at least not yet.

At this point I should make an inventory I suppose, because if I ever did manage to get to own her I suspected she would have to be returned in the same condition. Starting at the top: her two eyes to begin with were exactly the right distance apart, and her nose in between them was exactly the right length, and her cheek bones were prominent to exactly the right degree, and her lips were full of exactly the right fullness and were the right shade of pink and spoke exactly the right words at exactly the right time, and her neck and her collar-bones and her torso were all exactly the right size and shape and her exactly round breasts, I would have kissed them. Under the table I knew the good work continued with the hips and legs and feet.

Her feet her legs her hips her stomach her exactly round breasts and back up to the top again my eyes went, to where the beautiful head was.

Walter was trying his hardest to be the life and soul of the party. I was tongue-tied and the beer was making me feel somewhat worse for wear, but the presence of Colubrine on my right-hand side was enough to recharge me. So what did I do? I looked into my beer. I could feel my drunken cock clambering around in my lap trying to get out of my trousers and lay itself inside her and be surrounded by her, but I ignored it as much as is possible under the circumstances.

'What about a toast,' Walter said. 'To old friends, to new friends,' he said as he raised his glass. Colubrine raised hers.

'I'll drink to that,' she said, 'although I've fallen out with my old friends. One of them is a pig,' she continued, 'and the others just go along with him.'

'To your new friends, then,' said Walter.

'Hear hear!' said I.

'And fuck the pig,' Walter added, raising his glass again.

I put my hand on the table for Colubrine to take hold of if she needed some comfort. She looked ahead, glassy-eyed, thinking of the pig no doubt, and I wondered for a second if they had some kind of romantic involvement going on, her and the pig, and I felt a stab of jealousy. My cock ran for cover between my legs and I picked up my pint with the hand that had been left there for her use. I soon forgot it all though, all thoughts of the pig, as the drink wiped my memory clean of it, of him, and their possible relationship. Instead I thought about the beer I was holding in my mouth, growing warm and foul-tasting.

Walter excused himself: 'I'm going to see a man about a pig,' he said, and walked away in an untidy line through the crowds, laughing to himself.

I can't recall at this time the extent of our – I mean Walter and my – shared relationship with Colubrine. I think she was probably ignorant of me, but I certainly wasn't ignorant of her, and Walter wasn't ignorant of her either, but – and here's the thing – I suspected that if Walter knew anything about my feelings for her at this point he knew very little, because he was happy to leave us together, and this was something he would later be loath to do.

Okay, this is as far back as I can go, and indeed, what's the point of going back any further? I can only describe everything that happened to me after this point.

As soon as Walter was out of my sight I decided to take the lead and I said to her, 'I am a little besotted with you.'

Colubrine laughed charmingly.

'I admit it,' I added. 'I've seen you from afar and now that I have seen you close-up I can say that with certainty.'

'In that case,' she said – and she laughed a little again – 'why don't you give me a little kiss on the cheek?'

'Are you serious?' I asked.

'Of course,' she replied, charmingly again.

'That wouldn't be seen as an imposition?'

'No, go ahead,' she said and turned her face away from me.

I brought my lips into action, close to her face, puckering them up. But am I doing this for the sake of making a scene in front of the pig? I wondered, and as this thought suddenly entered my head, which was almost at the point of impact, I tried, at the same time, to see, out of the corner of my eye, whether I was performing in front of an audience. As a result of this my kiss struck more of a glancing blow, rather than it being a clear and honest statement of the true and loving feelings I was having for her at that moment.

In my defence, and to hide my blushing face, I said, 'You're safe with me.'

'Am I?' she asked, turning again to face me.

'I'm sitting on my hands,' I said, and I nuzzled against her shoulder.

When Walter returned he had more drinks.

'What's going on here?' he asked.

'You're a fool Walter,' I said, because I believed he was; I thought I had him fooled you see.

'I am,' he said. 'How could I ever have thought anything different?'

And he raised his glass again: 'To all the fools in all the world,' he said. 'And I am the king of them.'

Don't let me drink any more, I thought.

The next time Walter left us I took up where I had left off. Already I had a course of action in my mind. To begin with I said, 'If you really want to give him something to think about, why don't you give me a cuddle?'

'Give who something to think about?' she asked.

'The pig,' I said.

'I don't care about the pig,' she said.

'Of course,' I replied, my plan already in ruins about me.

'I thought you meant Walter,' she said.

'Give me a cuddle anyhow.' I said. 'I've recently had a piece of bad news.'

'Have you?' she asked.

'Yes,' I said, 'but I don't want to talk about it.'

'Come here then,' she said, and she pulled me onto her chest to give me some comfort. I climbed on happily, leaning over, so that in order to accommodate the new position I found myself in, I had to injure my back by twisting my spine. My fingers tickled at my buttocks, finding as it were a couple of free inches under there now that I had been lifted in my seat, and my eyes rolled in my head while my tongue hung out.

I could only take everything in – I mean mostly the smell of her, and the feel of her I suppose – through the ministrations of the muscles in my face as they set about moving independently of each other, as if I was groping her with my hands.

I thought, The pig's going to want to have a word with me about this, but I didn't care.

When Walter returned he said, as he sat back down, 'What's going on here then?'

She nudged me off, and I sprang back up into a sitting position, out of the glorious clinch we had shared, and in the process I injured my neck, such had been the shock of the sudden ascent; and the injury to my neck went with the injuries

I had already sustained, namely the twisted spine and the exhausted muscles down one side of my face and also my nearly broken fingers which were mid-tickle on my buttocks when I was suddenly forced to sit on them.

'You're more of a fool than I first thought you were, Walter,' I said with some venom.

'I am,' he said. 'I am. And I'd like to toast all the fools in all the world,' he said, 'and all the fools' friends who take them for fools.'

'I'll drink to that,' I said, raising my glass. Then I leaned across to Colubrine and whispered in her ear.

'This piece of bad news,' I said, 'it's the worst kind of bad news you can imagine.'

She looked at me and winked, and I tried to wink back but my face was still numb: the other eye, the other eye, I thought in a panic, but before I could act Walter said, 'For once I'd like to be in on the joke.'

'Ah,' I said, to let him know how good it was, from here in my superior position, to be in on the joke, only for Colubrine to say, 'There is no joke,' thus bringing me immediately back to earth; the whole sense of my being, and feeling, superior to Walter, was over with as quickly as it had begun.

At ten-thirty we were all in the lift together and on the fourth floor we all got out, us to return to our rooms, she intending to use the stairs to go down to her floor below.

When we found ourselves on our landing Walter invited her in for a nightcap before I could get a word in, and probably, seeing that there were two of us, she considered it safe to accept.

In Walter's room she sat on the bed and I sat next to her while Walter was looking around for the bottle of Scotch he had hidden.

I whispered to her, 'I want you I want you I want you.'

She sighed and rolled her eyes.

Finally Walter found what he was looking for on its side, under the bed, by reaching between our legs. He poured her a shot into the cup he took off the sink, which was the only cup in the room. I offered to go next door to fetch my cup but instead he sat on the chair and passed me the bottle.

'I was wrong about you,' Walter said to her.

He took the bottle out of my hand before I could drink anything from it, and leaned over to clink it against the side of her glass.

'What do you mean?' she asked.

'Nothing to get upset about,' he said. 'I was paying you a compliment.'

'I'm sure nothing you could do would upset me,' she replied.

He tried to get to his feet but had to sit back down.

'What is this muck anyhow?' she said after a while, holding up her glass, and Walter started to laugh.

'It's a fine single malt,' he said, 'and it makes you drunk.'

'I'm drunk already,' I said because I had begun to think I hadn't said anything for some time, and it wasn't that I was missing the sound of my own voice but I was afraid I might become invisible in the conversation.

'This makes you nonsensical then,' he said, 'but in a good way.

'A toast,' he added.

'No,' I said.

'No?'

'I'm sick of toasting,' I said.

'To the single malt,' he said, regardless.

'I've decided I don't like single malt,' she said.

He tried again to stand up, and after rocking backwards and forwards a couple of times he managed to get to his feet.

'Well would you like to dance then?'

He passed the bottle to me and held out his open hand in invitation.

'Why not?' she said. 'I love to dance. I love nothing more in the world.'

She put her glass on the table and took his hand. They held each other and swayed together like this. I imagined the feel of her body against mine and despite it all I could feel myself becoming erect. I was overcome with a wave of desire, or it might have been nausea, and in an effort to displace him and gain my rightful place I shuffled around until I managed to get to my feet and, approaching them, I said, 'Do you mind if I cut in?'

Walter released her and turned to me.

'Not at all,' he said, and he took me in his arms and began to spin me around the room.

As the drink began to rise back up in me I lashed out at him to release me. The bottle I was still holding in my hand caught him on the side of the face and he stumbled back and fell over the end of the bed, onto the floor.

Released now, and under my own unsteady orientation, I was unable to keep my footing. The room began to lurch around me. I fell on top of him and discovered I had continued to lash out, beating him about the face and arms as he put them up to protect himself. The bottle spun out of my hand and away under the table.

It was only a moment though, before my momentum forced me to roll off him and we lay side by side on the floor looking up at the ceiling. Colubrine was standing over us with her back to the door.

'I love you,' I said for good measure, and as a natural step on from all the previous assertions I had made. It gave Walter the opportunity to laugh at me again, it sounded more like a croak though, it rattled in his throat and then it either disappeared back down his gullet or it crept out silently onto his chin, unnoticed.

Colubrine opened the door and left. We lay side by side for a long time.

When I awoke from my snooze, Walter was silent beside me. I pulled myself upright using the edge of the bed and promptly reeled over to the sink and vomited into it. When I finished I found I was crying. The tears were running down my face. Colubrine had left the door open and the draught coming through it had stiffened my already-injured neck so that I could look neither left nor right. With my twisted back I was facing the wrong way.

As I passed Walter on the way out I gave his head another swift kick. He was a dead weight against the force of my boot.

I began to take the lift to the third floor on a regular basis because I had discovered that that was where Colubrine lived. I would get off to walk up to my landing, but it wasn't for the exercise of course, I was hoping to catch a glimpse of her coming or going.

One day I did see her; she disappeared into her room as I got off the lift. I remembered the courage I had been storing up for a moment like this and I called on it: I took every step from here to her door with one purpose in mind, which was to seduce her, and I knocked on the door.

I had also made all manner of plans for my opening speech in the weeks that I had been busy storing up the courage. One gave the other life: it was the courage that meant I would be standing at her door with the words in my mouth, and it was the opening speech that would provide the courage, the confidence that it would not be wasted when the door was opened. The words and the intentions tangled up in my mouth though, and when I saw Walter get off the lift while I was standing there I was not sorry to use it as an excuse to abandon the mission. I said it had taken me days to pluck up the courage, but suddenly seeing him there unsettled me and all the courage was immediately dissipated.

He was obviously spooked too, because he turned on his heel and made his way back down the corridor, the few feet he had travelled so far. I went after him, mainly because I was rattled.

I looked back and saw Colubrine standing outside her door watching us. I caught up with Walter outside the lift.

'Where are you going?' I asked him.

'Ah, wouldn't you like to know?' he said.

The lift was a long time in coming though, and we stood saying nothing for some time, except that Walter would occasionally mutter, half under his breath, 'Wouldn't you like to know,' as if he was afraid that what he saw as the strength of his stand was being dissipated into the thin air, even as we stood there.

It became ridiculous.

I looked again at Colubrine, who hadn't moved, and I raised my hand, which was an attempt at a wave; but it faltered and I lowered it again. I was going to call out, but I didn't do that either, I only reddened and was mortified: it was too late to go back to her. After all she had seen me choose him over her. If only I could have made out the look on her face.

When the lift doors finally opened I stepped inside thankfully, and we travelled down to the ground. I followed Walter in the direction away from the foyer towards the grounds, which were reachable only through a winding corridor that passed the kitchens and what I had been told were the staff quarters, past a long row of doors, until at the end we came out onto a broad patio with a low wall that separated it from the gardens. There were plastic tables and chairs on either side of us and each table had a furled umbrella sticking out of it like the idle sail on a boat on a windless day. Around the perimeter of the grounds were high trees and an unscaleable wall.

I followed him as he strode purposefully out into the blue light. Further away from the building, hidden slightly by the foliage, were tennis courts and a pool full of fish and lily pads and ducks.

I sat next to Walter on one of the benches. Other people sat around the pond and ate sandwiches. Behind us, the building was a huge edifice of red bricks and windows; from here I could appreciate the sheer size of it for the first time.

Walter stared ahead silently.

'I know I've been acting badly,' he suddenly said.

I had been watching a woman to our right breaking hunks of bread off her sandwich and throwing them into the pond for the ducks; I imagined a kind of intimacy with her that I had been missing; I was overcome by the look of childlike excitement on her face. The ducks fought over the bread as it turned to dough on the surface of the water.

Walter though was looking to me for some sort of response. I put my hand on his knee. I was aware that it was a false gesture.

The woman threw the last of her sandwich into the water, stood up, and walked towards us.

'Of course,' he said in response to my action, 'how can I have thought such a thing?' I looked at my hand on his knee. My knuckles were turning white with the pressure I was applying. There was a look of panic in Walter's eyes, but it was only momentary. Neither of us had a true grasp of the situation.

'I want to deal with it differently,' he said.

'Yes,' I said. 'You don't have to be jealous, Walter.'

Walter looked up, sucking in air. He willed the birds out of the trees but they didn't come.

I turned and watched the woman as she passed us. I attempted a smile. She hesitated and then smiled weakly back at me, before she continued on her way. I watched her until she was out of sight. I withdrew my hand from Walter's knee. Walter closed his eyes and wrung his hands in his lap.

'I have been suffering from visions,' he said at last, his eyes still tightly shut.

'What do you mean?' I asked him.

'I have been witness to signs that are sure-fire,' he continued. 'Somebody is telling me what to do.'

'Who?' I asked.

'Who?' He opened his eyes, turned, and looked at me as if I had punched him on the nose.

From now on he'll use this as an excuse for anything that causes disquiet between us, I thought; even at that moment I could see that, and of course this only incensed me further; with it he hopes to abdicate responsibility, I thought. And I already harboured all sorts of ill feelings towards him, especially in regard to my legitimate claim on Colubrine and his determination to thwart me, at first with constant distractions and then, when they didn't work, by setting himself up as my rival in love.

We sat there on the bench for a long time. Even from here I could see the fish coming up to the surface of the water. I saw their open mouths, or I imagined I did. For a second they hung on the lip between their world and ours, and then they quickly withdrew back into the water.

'What about these visions?' I asked him finally.

'What about them?'

'I don't know,' I said, 'what are they like?'

'Ha,' was all he said, as if I would never be able to understand, and that was going to be that on the subject of the visions.

'Mr D has assured me they are prophetic,' he said shortly afterwards.

'Why are you listening to anything Mr D says?' I asked him.

'I am all submerged action,' he said.

'According to Mr D?'

'He says I might think an action has taken place already, but it was never manifest in the outside world, it only existed inside me.'

'What action?'

'Stay away from the canteen,' he said.

'Why?'

'Just do as I tell you.'

'When? How am I supposed to eat?'

'I'll let you know.'

'Walter, what have you got in mind?'

'I can't tell you,' he said. 'You chose not to be a member of the revolutionary council.

'Of course you can still change your mind,' he added.

'I don't want anything to do with it,' I said.

'I've said too much already,' he said with some finality.

He got to his feet and looked down at me pityingly. Then he turned and strode off.

It started to play on my mind that perhaps my association, with Walter primarily but also with Mr D, was damaging my case. After all, I thought, the walls have ears. I couldn't believe the authorities didn't have some wind of what was going on.

This unease of course was manifest in my letters of complaint, as indeed were all of my thoughts and feelings. I wrote them daily, as I had a lot of time on my hands. Before I had either been with Walter or on the lookout for Colubrine. Now all my ties with him were strained and I was equally uncomfortable meeting her after the episode outside her door.

I began my latest letter of complaint: *First of all let me assure you I am still here,* and I continued on and on. It informed me at the end of the form that I was to attach any extra pages necessary and I began to staple sheet after sheet onto the back of the original pages.

I hate delay, I continued, *and while I am fully aware that you have many other duties to see to, I worry that you have forgotten me. I can't say it any clearer than that can I? At the last meeting I had with your representatives I was promised action. Where is it? I have waited ever since, with baited breath, but have received nothing, no action, no news of any action, nothing! I have also been assured that all these documents are received directly by yourself, and have never received any information from you, or anyone else who might work under you, to the contrary. I shall therefore continue to entreat you and hope that you might hasten my exit, as I have a connection to make. I can only hope that you understand my predicament. You can see how it is for me, can't you? You're a human being surely, and you have feelings yourself.*

Have you never felt trapped like this?

How did you come to be here? How did you come to be here yourself?

I wrote: *The other thing I want to bring to your attention by the way is this: you might hear news of a man fitting my description stirring up trouble around the place. I would like at this point to say this, that it isn't me! I would like to say that to you categorically.*

It is true I have been made aware that there are plans afoot, but I am not involved in any of them, in fact I have only distanced myself from them at every available opportunity. Please believe me.

I am, however, unfortunate enough to know who the trouble-makers are.

And here I named Walter and Mr D, as much for their own good as for mine.

I was hoping that this new direction might hurry through my claim.

Walter had already begun to complain that his visions had worsened by this time, or at least that they had become something else – it was a rapid decline – and he had to start taking tablets for headaches he was getting down one side of his face.

It started when he called out in the night. I got out of bed and went and knocked on his door. When he opened it he said, 'What is it?' I said, 'You were calling out.' 'Was I?' he said, 'I thought I was doing it in my dream.'

I had still been knocking for him in the mornings on the way to breakfast, but more often than not now he stayed in his bed and I would run into him later, in the day room.

Today though, he was looking particularly out of sorts. I feared the worst. I thought: Am I found out? Maybe I have been betrayed by somebody in officialdom.

He didn't look angry though, he looked exhausted; he was sat hunched over a pile of papers that were on the table in front of him. He seemed unable to read what was written on them.

'They've given me these to fill out,' he said, looking at the papers.

'What are they?' I asked.

'It's part of their conspiracy against me,' he said.

He let me look at them. 'It's only a formality actually.'

'Are you having problems?'

'Some,' although he'd said it was only a formality.

'What is it?'

He grimaced.

At this time of day the light was so bright that all the decorative lines that were intermittent on the wallpaper, that were more like perfectly straight cracks in the plaster, were bleached out of sight. The whole room in fact took on an otherworldly ambience. Walter was surrounded by light, and while it picked out the edges of him for particular attention, the rest of him, the meat in the middle, was somehow lost to shadow.

He was holding the questionnaire in front of his face, but I could see none of it was going in.

Finally, to cut short the silence, I asked him, 'Do you want me to read the questions out to you? I'll write your answers down for you if you like.'

He thought that was an idea. 'But I haven't been to school for years,' he said to make light of the situation, and he made a small noise that I presumed was an attempt at a laugh.

'Okay,' I said, shuffling the papers together on the tabletop in front of me, 'but let's get something straight from the start, shall we?'

'What's that?' he asked.

'Well,' I said, 'the point is I'm doing you a favour.'

'I wouldn't want that,' he replied, after a moment's pause.

'Why not?'

'Isn't that obvious?'

'Is it?'

'By the way,' he said, 'I haven't forgotten our little trip into town.' He smiled.

I smiled back.

'To be honest with you,' I said, 'that drip has become something of a comfort to me.' That wiped the smile off his face I can tell you, which I suppose had been my intention. I was aware though that it was going to be a one-sided battle – however much I would have liked to kid myself, he wasn't at all like his old self. It's the drugs they're feeding him, I thought. His hair, what little there was, he told me was falling out in clumps, the fire in his eye was put out, his ears lay close to the sides of his head.

I sharpened the pencil and I said to him, 'I'll put your name at the top of the paper, it helps me when I mark.' To this there was no reply from him.

'Now then,' I said, 'we can begin with adding.'

'Yes,' he said, 'I'm not afraid of adding.'

I said, 'Two plus two. Four.'

I wrote it down.

'You win,' he said, 'but I shall have my revenge on you yet.'

He smiled again. I smiled back at him, all as part of the game, obviously.

'Taking away,' I said. 'Two minus two. Nothing.'

I wrote it down.

'Now we're back to where we started from.'

'If you can't do the simplest sums...' I said.

'Shut up,' he said mockingly, as if really he considered himself a mathematical genius.

'Well what do you want me to start you with?'

'What do you mean?'

'If you're having trouble with these,' I said.

'Fuck you,' he replied. 'To start with, fuck you actually,' he added.

This was certainly uncharacteristic of him I admit, but it only fuelled my desire to humiliate him.

'I want you to write this down,' I continued. 'Tommy has two pennies.'

I wrote it down.

'No, Tommy only has one penny.'

I wrote it down.

'It's his last penny. And Timmy takes it.'

'Tommy has no pennies!' he said quickly.

'That isn't what I'm asking. Why did Timmy take the penny?'

'How do I know?' he said.

'You do know that it isn't right?'

'I can't be expected to know that just from what you told me,' he protested.

'Well this is where your education truly begins,' I replied while I thought: Let him protest.

'I have a set of numbers, that's all I have,' he said.

'Timmy goes to hell for stealing the penny,' I said.

'You bastard,' he said.

I could see I was beginning to get him riled.

'I want you to write this down,' I said. 'If Tammy has one penny and Sammy takes it, how many pennies has Tammy got left? She has no pennies.'

I wrote it down.

'These are easy ones to start off with.'

'Yes.'

'Only you seem to be having trouble.'

'No.'

'Are you sure?'

'You fucker,' he said.

'Ah.'

'Yes,' he said. 'I mean it.'

'Good,' I said. 'Let's do something else.'

'Okay,' he replied.

'I want you to write this down.'

I paused, the pen poised over the paper. He looked at the pen in my hand.

'Underneath this honest face,' I said, 'I'm a liar a coward and a cheat.' I meant him of course, as I was still writing all this down under his name.

'That isn't maths.'

'Not everything is as it looks,' I said.

'I'm not writing that,' he said.

'I insist,' I said, and I wrote it down.

'Don't write it,' he said.

'You haven't even got an honest face.'

'Don't write that either.'

I wrote it. I brandished the pen like a sword.

'What have you grown up into?'

'A man,' he said.

'What's a man?'

'A man is a man.'

'You haven't learnt anything,' I said, 'you've grown up into a monster.'

'Fuck you.'

I was surprised at the way our conversation was spinning out: something was welling up in me, I couldn't contain it; his responses were like the thrashings of a dying animal, I had him where I wanted him.

'I want you to write this down,' I said. 'If Jimmy has two pennies, no, one penny, one penny…if Jimmy has one penny, what should he do with it?'

'You keep on asking me the same question,' he said.

'I do not.'

'You do.'

'It's a different question every time,' I said. 'And besides what the fuck do you know about Jimmy?'

'I think I've had enough of this for today,' he said.

'I'll decide that!'

We sat and looked at each other; I was perhaps grimacing at him.

I wanted to tell him it was all about Colubrine. I was angry that he had tried to steal her out from under my nose. I was angry about the dance. I was also angry he had been ignoring me.

'I used to know a man who suffered like you,' I said.

'I don't suffer,' said Walter. But I knew he did. I looked at him. I looked away. I looked at him again. He had a tear in his eye.

'I have all these things to say,' he said, 'but I don't get to pass them on to anyone any more. I'm full of words. I'm constipated with it.'

I said, 'I only want you to speak to me again.'

He said, 'Of course that's what I want.'

I said, 'Can't we put everything else behind us?'

'Yes,' he said.

'Can't it be like it was before?'

And he said, 'That's what I want.'

We sat and looked at each other for some time. He attempted to express a conciliatory tone by some slight movement of his eye or mouth, and in response to this I tried to beat his conciliatory tone with a better conciliatory tone of my own. A conciliatory tone though is not something you can easily express, when you try to, in the arch of an eyebrow perhaps or a curl of the lip, and there was never going to be a winner.

'I haven't thought about things like this for a long time,' he said.

'What things?'

'Any things,' he said. 'I don't know, significant moments. Three days after I was born my father took my hand and we walked out of the hospital side by side. He put me straight on the bus and said, You're on your own now kiddo.'

This was the first time Walter had reached out to me in a long time.

'Mr D has betrayed me,' he said finally.

'Has he?' I asked.

'He was never going to help me,' he added.

I had won then.

At least it felt like I had won. Mr D had been exposed as the charlatan I had predicted he was at the start.

'As far as he was concerned I was inviting disaster,' Walter said. Actually on this, I thought, he had a point.

'He said I had a preoccupation with trying to change the world, which was a hoax as far as he was concerned,' Walter said.

So Mr D had proved to be fair-weather, and the whole sorry revolution had come tumbling down with his abdication.

'Anybody who is in the process of trying to change the world, he said, knows it's a hoax too,' Walter said, 'and makes themselves miserable thinking about it.

'I'm miserable,' Walter said, 'but not because of that.'

I reached out my hand to him and he took it. It occurred to me that this was my trump card; in the midst of this confusion of conciliatory twitches and blinking eyes, a hand outstretched is a masterstroke, and as is often the case, the masterstroke comes intuitively.

We both wept a little, he perhaps for the incessant pains in his head and me for the mildly troubling ache that occasionally flared up in my heart. And I loved him again at that moment. If I had hated him a moment before, I loved him again now, and yet I felt I could do nothing to help him; he was crippled by the pains in his head and the drugs he was taking to try and alleviate them.

I had a picture of him in my mind. He was standing with his fist in the air as a gesture of rebellion. That's how I shall remember you, I thought.

I didn't want to let go of his hand.

'I thought they were multiple-choice,' he said finally, nodding at the questionnaire I was still holding in my other hand.

I could see they were. I pulled myself together. I said, 'Yes, the answers to the following questions are either a, b, c or d.'

He said, 'We should get this over with, after all it's lamb chops for tea.'

My throat was suddenly dry.

'Could I have a sip of your water before we start?' I asked.

'A sip,' he said. 'I need it to take my pills.'

I took a sip and returned to the questionnaire.

'Question 1,' I began. 'Which of these statements is, in your experience, most true?: a) If M has followed the same recommended route as N, does it mean they have made the same journey?; b) M may have made the trip solely on N's recommendation but that may only be because, of all the recommendations given to M, N's best fitted M's idea of what a successful recommendation should include; c) Any recommendation is only successful if the recommender, N, touches on the point in the recommendee, M, that is most ready to receive it. Good conveyance of a recommendation, in truth, requires more effort, as there are more than a hundred ways a recommendation can be altered in the conveying of it, while there remains only one way for an exact copy to be passed on; any other way is not a copy; d) If M is drawn to N's recommendation, it may not be because of the thing N recommends necessarily, but because of the way it is recommended. It is the success of the conveying of the recommendation that guarantees its prolonged lifespan; I mean how close it is to the original recommendation.'

I looked at him. He couldn't look at me. I don't think he was avoiding my gaze but he wasn't lifting his head up either. Maybe he was exhausted with it all. His hands were now under the table out of my sight.

'A, b, c or d?' I pressed him for an answer.

'Fuck it,' he said with finality.

'You're right,' I said. And then after a pause, I said, 'What shall I tick then?'

'Tick them all,' he said.

'I can't,' I said.

'Fuck it,' he said again.

'We can come back to that one. Question 2,' I said after a moment's pause. 'If given the choice, select: a) A babbling brook, a super highway, a cloudless sky, the Great Western; b) A romantic comedy, a horror, a thriller or the Great Western.' I paused. He was looking at me as if he was asking me to spare him his life.

'Could I take another sip of your water?' I asked him.

'No,' he said, 'I told you I need it for the pills.'

'Won't they give you a drop more?' I asked.

'Okay okay,' he shouted. 'Have it then!'

After a moment, during which nothing was shared (only evil looks) I said, 'I was only trying to help.'

'You were only trying to help?'

'Yes,' I said.

He paused and then he said, 'How could I have thought anything different?' And after a while he added, 'It's the headaches.'

'They're no better, then?' I asked.

'No.'

He was on a regime of pills that were making him feel sick in the mornings, apathetic in the afternoons and devil-may-care in the evenings. He told me there was no real progress being made and he had become frightened that he was suffering from something more serious, perhaps a brain tumour. He said, 'I'm afraid of every little pain.'

It takes him five minutes to take his pills. He sets them up on the tabletop in a line. He takes them one after another, at first the elbow at 90°, then the movement of the hand from the table – with the pill clutched between the thumb and the forefinger – and back again, now empty, having deposited the pill in the mouth.

And what's his other hand doing? It holds the glass of water to one side and slightly away from the mouth, like a moon orbiting his head, and as the pill is deposited in the mouth the head turns slightly towards the glass and the arm swings the glass in so that the two meet and are tipped backward in unison ...and then are tipped forward again – now the glass swinging away and the head forward to receive the next pill, that by now is rising towards it in the other hand...and so on.

How can a mind that is so baffled conceive of and then repeat this kind of choreography? It's beautiful, like a machine. But when it's finished, when all the pills are gone, the body crumples again, as if the power to it has been cut.

Throughout the rest of the visit we sit facing each other, mostly. I am not sure he cares whether I am there or not.

When it was clear our encounter had completely exhausted him – the whites of his eyes had filled up with tiny red blood vessels – he told me he wanted to lie down.

I took him back to his room and put him into his bed.

'Will you sit with me for a while?' he asked.

'I'm happy to,' I said.

I knew he certainly planned to keep me by his bedside all night because he probably sensed I had it in my mind to go and see Colubrine – somehow the strength I needed to face her had returned to me. I was suddenly aware of my powers. I had triumphed over Mr D, without even joining battle; he had surrendered, and I had Walter now, at my mercy. I sat by the bed and stroked his head. I stroked it like I'd never stroked a head before. Yes.

Because I was putting everything I had into my stroking, and because stroking was another one of my talents, I wasn't surprised when his eyes were almost immediately heavy and I saw him struggling to keep them open. I continued to stroke his head and then, to finish him off, I began to hum the lullabies my mother had sung to me as a child. He gritted his teeth. He tried to thrash about but I had tucked the blankets in so tight, he was unable to move.

Finally he closed his eyes and I could see the muscles in his jaw relax. His mouth gaped. Now all I could see inside it were the words he hadn't wanted to say to me, but were there nonetheless, and I was shocked to see them because I had mistakenly thought him defeated as well, they said something like, *If you go to her that's it with us*.

For a moment I sat there, and then I felt a rage stirring in me that I hadn't known was there, but that, at the same time, I had conjured up, to stir me into action. I had placed his teeth in order to spell out what I wanted to see.

'I've come to apologise,' I said straight away, as soon as Colubrine opened her door to me.

'This isn't going to take long, is it?' she asked.

'No,' I replied.

'Go on then,' she said.

'What?' I asked.

'Say what you've come to say.'

'I've just said it,' I said. 'I wanted to say how sorry I was.'

'What have you come to apologise for anyway?' she asked me.

'I made a fool of myself in Walter's room,' I said.

'You're not apologising for knocking on my door the other week and running off?' she asked.

'No. Yes. That as well,' I said, flustered.

'Come in,' she said. And a second later I was standing inside her room, the door still open behind me. She had walked into the centre of the room to stand by the table.

Her room wasn't any different from mine except that it had

a few feminine touches. She had two chairs, one by the desk and one by the side of her bed. She stopped and turned round to look at me. She smiled. When she told me I could sit down I sat on the chair by the desk and she pulled up the other chair and put it beside mine. Then she offered me a drink.

Soon we were sitting side by side, each with a gin and tonic. While she'd been making it I had sat in silence. When she sat down and gave me the drink I'd hoped to have thought of something I could say to her but my mind was a blank. I took a big swig and I tried to hasten the journey of the alcohol to my brain by thinking harder and faster than normal, because I remembered how much looser my tongue had been before when I had been under the influence of beer. I also recalled though, that it had been the drink that caused me to embarrass myself, so I determined to seek out the safest line somewhere between the two.

We drank in silence. I knew that something was going to happen. I was confident, I felt my powers still in me; I had come here because I had vanquished all my enemies today already.

'I don't know whether you've noticed,' I began, 'but I've been following your case with a great deal of interest.'

'Have you?' she asked.

'I have indeed. And this is because I want the best of possible resolutions for you, I mean re:...actually,' I said, 'what is it you'd like?' I was already losing my way.

'You can do something for my case?' she asked.

'Not exactly,' I replied.

'What do you mean? What can you do?'

'Nothing,' I said.

'You can't help me?'

'I mean I've been watching you,' I said, 'I mean...' She knew what I meant. 'You know what I mean,' I said. She was playing with me. 'Let me put it another way...' I said, but I was distracted because suddenly she was moving. I watched her take a sip of her drink. I watched her throat contract. Her lips close. After they had opened they closed. She held the glass up and looked for a moment at the liquid in it, and then slowly she lowered the glass and she held it between her hands in her lap.

She looked at me for a minute and then she swilled the remains of her gin and tonic around in her glass and drank it down in one. She took my nearly-empty glass out of my hand and put it, with her glass, on the floor by the side of her chair.

'You're not so bad really are you?' she said as she ran her hands down her thighs to straighten the material of her skirt.

'You might not be what I'd call handsome but I've been thinking I could get used to you,' she said, and she took hold of my hand and put it against her cheek.

This was better than anything I had imagined.

We sat like this for a long while, with my arm stretched just far enough to make it uncomfortable for me to hold the position.

I shunted my chair forward a few inches.

The door was still open, which didn't make me feel any more comfortable; I was sure somebody would pass by and stop to look in. (I wondered if she worked best in front of an audience because in the bar hadn't there been the presence of the pig hanging over us?)

In the end this position, me with my hand on her cheek, held no meaning for either of us. I was like the boy with his finger in the crack in the dyke who forgets what he's standing there for and goes home, and I daydreamed that she was like the dyke who had all this pressure building up against the crack that I had my finger in and maybe that's why I took my finger out so that I could release all the pressure, which in this case was passion, but I doubted it.

I noticed the light in here was different than it was in my room. Looking at the shadows on the wall cast by the bedstead I would have said, in my room about then, it was four-thirty, but I was sure it couldn't be as late as that, or else I had been sitting in that position for over an hour.

Anyhow, whatever, the light had yellowed somewhat.

Colubrine finally moved the hand off her face and put it on her breast. I sat up straighter to concentrate. Then she put her own hand on my hand on her breast and asked, 'What can you feel?'

Finally I said, 'It's soft under there isn't it?'

She looked at me as if that was the wrong answer.

This position we now found ourselves in, me with my hand on her breast, was something she had been building up to, in the time we had sat with my hand on her cheek, I realised, and I had been wasting my time thinking about the bloody light and what time it was and getting ahead of myself thinking about the boy with his finger in the crack of the dyke and I knew my mood was totally out of sync with hers, so I tried desperately to catch up. 'I can't imagine,' I said first of all, to try and buy myself some time. 'I've thought about this all the time but I still can't imagine.'

But this didn't elicit a different response from her either.

'Just think,' I added, 'if we could stay like this for ever.' Will that do? I wondered.

'Is anything broken?' she asked finally.

'Broken?'

'Bruised then?'

'What's going to be broken?' I asked.

'My heart,' she said. 'Can you feel it pounding?'

'Yes.'

'Only I can't feel it beating at all.'

Did she want the heart to be beating? I wondered, or would she have preferred it if the passion had stopped it dead in its tracks?

'Yes,' I repeated, with little or no conviction though; I wanted to make sure it could be taken as an answer for both of these scenarios.

'Can you?' she asked. 'Can you feel it beating? Only I can't feel anything at all.'

'No, it's beating away all right,' I said.

She tipped her head to one side.

'Shouldn't I be able to feel something?' she asked, her voice cracking slightly.

'Give it a minute,' I said.

'It isn't pounding, I know that much. I think it's stopped beating altogether,' she said.

At this point I tried to think about what was under my hand and not be distracted too much by the conversation; I had a growing feeling that the whole thing was going to be short-lived and I decided I should make the most of it while I still had the chance. So I sought out the shape of her nipple beneath all those layers of material, but my hand had gone almost dead.

At the same time as I was concentrating on taking my pleasure I could sense she was becoming bored, so I also felt a need to continue talking to her, to distract her, otherwise the whole thing would come to an even more premature end, and so I said, 'I think you've just been thinking too much about it.'

'What are you taking about?'

'Well…'

'I think it's probably stopped beating out of a general lack of interest,' she said.

'I think you've thought about it so much, it's forced not to live up to your expectations.'

'If I fancied you,' Colubrine said, 'surely I'd be able to feel something. Wouldn't I?'

'Not necessarily,' I said.

'No, I would, I know I would.'

'Shall I move it around then?' I asked.

'No,' she said, 'that would be too much.'

'The whole thing is still in your mind and you've got to get it down into your body,' I said, but I could sense that I was beginning to let my impatience creep into my voice – no, not so much impatience – what was it? I was desperate I suppose.

'How do I do that?' she asked.

'Well,' I said, 'you have to push it. Oh good god, close your eyes and concentrate on my hand.'

Colubrine closed her eyes. I closed my eyes. I shunted my chair a few more inches closer to hold my wrist with my other hand, to support it, because by now it had started to ache terribly. Colubrine opened her eyes at the sound of the chair legs on the lino.

'Is your arm aching?' she asked.

'No.'

'Why are you holding it like that, then?' she asked.

'Can't you feel anything yet?'

'No,' she replied, curtly. 'And if your arm's aching you obviously aren't enjoying it either.'

'You can't feel it properly through all your bloody clothes,' I said, 'what if we take off a few layers?'

'No!'

'You're not concentrating,' I said, I almost shouted it actually. 'Close your eyes.' I felt her slipping further away from me. She closed her eyes for a matter of seconds before opening them again and moving my hand off of her.

'It's no good,' she said. By which time I had become desperate.

'What if I cupped it?' I asked, making a clumsy swoop at her bosom, a lunge I should call it, which missed because she leaned back out of my way as if she had had a premonition of what was coming.

'I don't love you,' she said, 'and that's that. I've been kidding myself. I can think about the pleasure I'm supposed to be feeling but that's no good to me.'

'That's what I mean,' I said, 'don't think about it.'

She stood up.

'Where are you going?' I asked her as I also got to my feet. 'Can I come?'

She sat back down. I sat back down opposite her again. We had taken up almost exactly the same positions as before but all the intimacy had completely gone out of the situation. We could easily have been enemies facing each other across a distance of two hundred metres or so.

'The fact is I don't love you and I can see that now,' she said. 'I was hoping that I would feel something, if not coming from inside me, then at least something coming out of you that I could hold on to. But I didn't feel anything coming out of you,' she said, 'only desperation.

'If only you'd do something,' she added.

I felt then that I had to make an audacious attempt to rescue the situation so I took up this position: I leant forward from the waist, at say 45°, and I bowed my head; my right hand I placed on my right knee with the elbow scooped out and up, making a square – with the forearm, the upper arm, the thigh and the side of my torso forming the four sides; the thumb and forefinger of the left hand I made into pincers that gripped the top of my nose, my brow I furrowed as heavily as I was able to furrow it with my conscious mind.

In other words I made of myself a picture of dejection, sorrow and self-pity.

After holding the position for a moment, to gain maximum effect, I said, 'They're sending me away though, Colubrine,' in a voice like that, that was very close to tears. I looked up to see what effect this new information had had on her, because she had been silent since I'd said it.

'When?' she asked, when she was aware my eyes had settled on her.

'I don't know,' I said, 'as soon as possible, they say.'

'Well, isn't that a good thing?'

'What do you mean?'

She was obviously talking about me getting out of the place and so I said, 'Yes it is,' and then I added, 'but I shall miss you.'

It was very dark by now. There was a grey light coming in off the landing (her door was still open), but it struggled to get more than a couple of feet into the room.

We sat for a while and neither of us said anything. Then she started to pick at her nails and the skin around her nails – I think firstly because she was bored, but also I think because somehow she felt that the dark had made her invisible. Or thirdly, and this is the worst of all, she had forgotten I was there.

The next morning I took Walter out into the garden. He came with me without any complaint; I helped him to dress and I half carried him down in the lift, his arm slung around my shoulder.

It started to rain though, almost as soon as we sat down on one of the benches. I had seen the clouds so I shouldn't have been surprised. All the other people took cover; they disappeared inside. I turned to Walter and was ready to carry him back indoors but he was happy to feel the drops on his face; they ran down his cheeks like tears. Soon we were alone. I was happy about this because I felt time was running out. I didn't know what that meant, it was just a feeling; as if I had the sense something had to be addressed, the something that had come between us. Actually I knew I didn't want to lose him. My encounter with Colubrine had brought me to my senses; I knew now that salvation did not lie in that direction.

What sort of a man am I, then? I was bouncing between the two of them, Walter and Colubrine, like a top, but I didn't care. That isn't true. If it could have turned out differently with Colubrine then I would have sided with her, probably; I had to side with one of them I suppose, but that was only because of Walter's intransigence.

I knew I couldn't see Colubrine again. I had returned to my room the night before humiliated, and this morning I had woken up with a clear head, as if from a deep black sleep.

As far as Walter knew I had been sitting at his bedside all night.

I decided I wouldn't tell him anything about my visit to see Colubrine, I would allow him to think I had made a sacrifice for the sake of our friendship, and this despite the fact I'd always believed she was the only woman for me. I'd tell him this. Wouldn't he be indebted to me for that? I wasn't thinking entirely straight though, remember I was also grieving the loss of her.

We sat there in silence. I'm not quite sure why nothing was said.

It soon stopped raining.

Then I saw Mr D was walking towards us. He isn't walking like a defeated man, I thought. He stopped and stood in front of Walter.

'I've been looking for you everywhere,' he said, and he cast a dirty look in my direction because he knew it was me that had spirited Walter away out here.

'It's raining,' he said. It wasn't, of course. It had stopped.

'What are you doing out here, anyway?' he asked.

'Getting a bit of fresh air,' Walter mumbled.

'Yes,' I added.

'Are you coming?' Mr D asked.

Leave him alone, I wanted to say. Walter raised his head though and looked at Mr D for the first time.

'He isn't talking to you,' I said to Mr D, defiantly.

'Of course he is,' he replied. 'Aren't you Walter? You're talking to me, aren't you?'

Walter smiled a bit. Mr D helped him to his feet.

'I'll see you later,' Walter said to me.

'Where are you going?' I asked.

Walter tapped the side of his nose conspiratorially and Mr D led him away.

I had a dream and in this dream I woke up with an overwhelming sense that today was the day I was going to complete my mission.

Everything had taken on a new sheen: the lights were brighter; the sun shining through the tiny window high in the wall at the end of the corridor lit up the lino on the floor, so that it reminded me of an ice rink.

I took the lift down and when I arrived in the foyer there was nobody about. I walked out into the car park and from there I walked into town and took a bus from the station.

I went in search of the man I had been instructed to find. His house was somewhere in the suburbs. I had it noted on the instructions I had been given. I had to walk the last couple of miles when I got off the bus.

At this point I apologise to myself for the brevity of the narrative. It's not the way I would like to have told it, but nonetheless it has all the makings of a wonderful story. So, it is a story. I told myself this in the dream.

And in this new place the sun was shining, the suburbs were sprawled across the hillside overlooking the ocean, all the houses were painted white and each had a square of green lawn in front of it. My legs were light and I made short work of the walk. People waved at me as I passed. I couldn't wipe the grin off my face, I didn't want to. I am happy, I thought. I am happy with my new haircut, the women wink at me, I am happy with my weight and the cut of my clothes. I see the houses on either side of me might be empty so I furnish them, the people in them fill out the clothes I take for them from the wardrobes; they have fifteen-second lives and then, when I have passed, they disappear and their houses disappear or they are consigned to some place in my memory where I can fetch them out again if I ever find myself in this neighbourhood again.

I think briefly about all the people. I consider their lives. As far as lives go, some were satisfying, while many were not. Even as I made them, I was unable to let them live in peace, I don't know why.

The man I am sent to meet is waiting for me. He says nothing to ruin my day but somehow instils in me the information that I have been sent to collect. I turn around and walk out into the sunshine.

And I can recount the return trip succinctly in a single line.

At first then I am enchanted by the simplicity of the transaction as has been described to me, the ease with which my purpose – to collect information from the man – had been fulfilled without a hitch. I congratulated myself actually, in the dream, for the invention. But my contentment proved to be short-lived, it wasn't long before something about the story started to irritate me, and it was this: while at first it might have seemed like simplicity itself, this little adventure, it was in truth far from that. The fact I'd had to walk the last two miles seemed to me superfluous to requirements. Why not move my final destination closer to the station, I asked myself? Since it had been an uncluttered expedition in every other respect, surely this was an unnecessary tax on my tired legs. These are the things that should have been taken into account when the whole thing was constructed, I thought.

And this was only one of the problems I had with it.

Other problems I had were to do with my acknowledging the organisation that was necessary to make the story at all convincing; how to make the whole journey run smoothly, that was the thing. I decided the only answer to this was that someone would have to be there ahead of me, to smooth out any potential problems; I mean all these women waving at me over their garden fences for a start, what the hell could all that have pointed to? It pointed to the fact that they would have to have been briefed, not only the women but anybody else I might have encountered on this route.

This realisation, though, only opened up countless other possibilities to me. If it wasn't a secret part of myself that was ahead of me working as an agent to warn those I was about to meet, then it had to be someone else, and by involving a second agent surely any hopes of keeping the exercise simple were dashed.

Anyway, perhaps I was interested in all this pretentious self-ruminating and perhaps I wasn't, perhaps I couldn't care less, but if I was interested, I wasn't interested because it was real, so I figured out I must have been interested for some other reason, and I certainly couldn't recognise what that reason might be at that moment.

I say it wasn't real because I was sitting there in the dream, watching events and judging them, but I was still judging them as if they were all real, which is where the confusion began to come into it; I couldn't be in two places at once, I thought: in the dream, and on the outside of the dream looking in. And then to make matters even more complicated there was the real me that was asleep in my room making the whole thing up.

The next morning I got up and knocked for Walter as I used to do, but hadn't been doing, and somebody else, who knew nothing about him, opened the door.

Alarmed, I went down to see if he was in the day room but he was nowhere to be found.

I looked everywhere for him and asked anyone I met who might have known him if they had seen him, but nobody had.

It was as if he had disappeared off the planet.

All the missed opportunities (we had never made it into town), the cross words, the days when we weren't talking to each other, came back to haunt me: I sat in the day room and they all passed in front of me, one by one. When I had castigated myself enough in my own opinion and I once again began to think more about Walter than about myself, I sought out Mr D as a last resort, to see if Walter had spoken to him.

He was seemingly unconcerned. He said he hadn't seen him. He also said he wouldn't be surprised to hear the worst.

'What do you mean by that?'

'You look tired,' he said and then he invited me in for a cup of tea.

I wrote: *To whom it may concern: You have the wrong man. The man you should have is called Mr D. Believe me. If you have Walter, wherever you have Walter, let me tell you he is not capable of causing any kind of serious trouble, even though he might fancy himself as a bit of a revolutionary. I can't believe that, if he's been* saying things like that to you, you could possibly believe him.

All the plans he had he has only recently had and I can tell you the reason for this: it is because he was manipulated by Mr D. I know it now.

In the days since Walter's disappearance I have been visiting Mr D on a regular basis, in order that I can bring the truth to you. (I have been relaxing on his Chesterfield; I love to feel the cold leather on the palms of my hands, and I won't deny that I have, for fleeting moments, imagined a lifetime here, in the comfort of this room, practising meditating on the taste of a cup of Oolong at Mr D's knee, but there are things you should know.)

The innards of his cutlery drawers are lined with flowered paper, and the knives and forks are free to go where they please, I mean there is no tray separating the spoons from the knives and the knives from the forks. I am no expert on cutlery, or the movement of cutlery – except in my hand from the plate to the mouth – but I want to bring it to your attention because you should see something in this: a man like Mr D wouldn't just let the cutlery run loose in his drawers.

He also told me this story: 'When I lived in dorms I used to sit on my bed when everyone else had gone out onto the streets for the day, because it was the only time I could get any peace and quiet. Once you've lived somewhere like that, your place becomes the most important thing in your life. But then this lunatic turned up and he ruined it all, because he decided to stay in too, and he was in the bed opposite me. So I never had any peace after that, and I thought he might be dangerous because he had that look in his eye that could have been insanity. While I did the crossword he'd sit on his bed across from me and stare, without inhibition or fear of offending me. I always hold the pen at arm's length because I'm afraid I might jab it in my eye, like this,' and he showed me what he meant by holding his arm out. 'So one day I asked him what he was staring at, and he said he was looking into the middle-distance. What do you mean by the middle-distance? I asked him. Was this middle-distance at some point equidistant between his bed and mine? I wondered. So to test the validity of his statement I would wiggle the pen at the end of my arm, which remained much closer to me, and certainly not equidistant between me and him, and watch for any movement from his eyes. A crude method I admit, but it was the best I was able to do at the time. Anyway I swear that often I would see his head bob to the left or the right, he was clearly pondering a spot on my side of the point of equidistance, but of course he always denied it, he told me that he was in fact nodding off, that because he couldn't sleep in the night he often took a nap in the morning or in the early afternoon. The whole place was a pigsty, the dorms I mean. I only had the bed and a small chest of drawers next to it, it wasn't even a chest of drawers actually it was a cabinet, a small cabinet. I kept my tooth-brush in it, in a glass. There was a kitchen with a stinking fridge and a single gas ring that was encrusted with burnt scraps of food, so I wouldn't go near it. I would only eat fruit or dry bread, and this made me shit three times a day. Meanwhile in the evenings I was *reduced to collecting pots in the Miner's Arms. I was paid in beer and this made me shit four times a day. I was growing weaker and weaker by the minute. So I decided I had only a few short weeks if I was going to keep enough strength in me to kill him. I bought a knife with my last few quid. I hid it under my mattress and waited for the right moment to use it on him. But he never slept. If I got out of my bed he would sit up. My nerves were shattered. I would hobble off to the john. By now, what with the excess of fruit, the beer and the nerves, I was shitting five times a day. Anyway one day I woke up and he was gone, as suddenly as that, so I threw the knife in the canal.'*

On another occasion he said to me, 'You are a man who has not achieved your potential,' and of course I secretly thought he was right. He had a talent to hit it right on the spot. My life lay behind me like a room with all the furniture turned over.

'What are your dreams?' he asked me, and I thought: how can I say the right thing, the thing that will please him most?

The rest of my time was becoming increasingly out of focus. I found I was very tired all of the time and I couldn't attribute it to anything in particular.

Mr D shut the cutlery drawer with a clatter and spooned heaped teaspoons from the caddy into the pot. I breathed into my chest and my belly, and my arms and legs. I was sitting in a high-backed chair because Mr D wouldn't let me sit on his new Chesterfield any more, not since I spilt tea on it. It had also been forbidden to even mention Walter's name during one of our tea-mornings.

Whatever.

Even if I wasn't particularly comfortable I must have dozed, because I had the sense I was waking up when he held out to me a thin bone-china cup; and when I took it from him I felt only the heaviness of the tea itself; the liquid in the cup was still moving in an anti-clockwise circle, in the direction he had stirred it. (Is that a bad sign?) The perfume of it had mixed with the air; as I lifted the cup up to my nose I was almost overcome with it. The first thing I always did was look for somewhere I could put the cup down.

'Drink your tea,' he said.

He poured himself a cup and then he brought the pot and his cup to the coffee table and sat down on the easy chair opposite me.

'By the way,' he said, 'all that business with the man I wanted to kill in the dormitory...'

'Yes?'

'Well I was afraid you'd misunderstood my intentions for telling you.'

'No,' I replied, and then, 'What is it?' I asked, because I could sense he had left something unsaid. I wondered aloud: Did he not feel he could tell me? 'After all,' I said, 'we could still count on each other as friends.'

He said we could, he hoped we could. He was covering the pot with the tea cosy.

'I suppose everybody has wanted to kill somebody at some point in their lives,' he said, and I was sure now that he was going to go on and tell me that he hadn't thrown the knife in the canal at all, but had plunged it into this poor man's heart.

'But for me it was doubly resonant,' he said, 'because there were murders once in my family.'

'Really?' I said.

'Yes. My great-grandfather poisoned his wife.'

'Your great-grandmother,' I said foolishly.

'Yes, and he was supposed to have taken after his father, who it was said suffocated his wife with a pillow while she was sleeping. This only came to light though when the poisoning had been discovered and my grandfather was looking to avoid punishment. You see, he said it was in him from birth.'

'Ah.'

'Let me assure you,' he continued, 'I'm not telling you this to get any kind of reaction out of you.'

For the life of me I couldn't think of the reaction he might have been looking for.

'So you can see why I would have some concerns about the murderous thoughts I had been having myself?'

'Yes.'

'Worse than that,' he continued, 'I used to charm women on first dates by telling them that story. You see they pitied me, while at the same time appreciating the effort I was expending to overcome my past. They thought of me as strong and sensitive, so a sort of intimacy was forged,' he said, 'but it was false. I had not laid myself bare at all,' he went on to say, 'although they thought I had. You see it was a story I'd told a hundred times before and it had lost all its magic for me.'

'Yes,' I said, and after that he stopped talking. There was a long silence until finally he said, 'You're shocked.'

'No,' I said.

'You are.'

It's true I was shocked, but only slightly. No, I was exhilarated more than anything, exhilarated that he had been able to confide in me.

'I can only tell you,' he said, 'because I have come to terms with it myself.'

It all seemed utterly unbelievable to me; looking back on our encounters to date, the only time I had ever seen any hint of a murderous lineage in him was when I asked him for milk in my Earl Grey.

I might not have liked him, but I never thought he was a killer.

He stood up and went to the cupboard to get some biscuits and I began to examine all the feelings I'd had for him during the few months I had known him; I remembered the instinct I had had about him when I first met him, and all the conversations I had had with Walter when I had spent the whole time damning him. Then it suddenly occurred to me that maybe I had not been damning enough. After all, I had always been terrified of his bone china, hadn't I? I had always handled it so carefully (and here I was now, taking my attention away from it; it had been there in my hand all along, unsupervised). I put it back on the table.

I wondered next if it was perhaps him I was afraid of, and not the crockery at all (this seemed like a sensible course for my thoughts to take, bearing in mind the new information I had just been given), and maybe I had been guilty of attributing the fear to the wrong thing; as it was, I always left the cup and saucer on the coffee table in front of me, and leant forward to take the occasional sip, while he held the cup and saucer in his hands like this – the saucer in one hand, the cup in the other, against his chest as if it was a newborn infant, and when he sipped he held his little finger out.

Mr D sat down again with a plate of biscuits. I took a ginger nut and put the whole thing in my mouth because of the crumbs.

'Why are you telling me this?' I asked.

'I'm trying to tell you that none of us are bound to do anything we don't want to do,' he said.

'Of course,' I said.

He sat and looked at me as I chewed and I knew he had something else he wanted to say to me. 'Is that it?' I asked him.

'No,' he said. 'My great-grandmother and great-grandfather conceived of Gareth in the first happy days of their union,' he said, 'and Gareth, whom they came to call Gary out of familiarity and fondness, married my grandmother.

'Their son, Mike, whom they came to call Michael out of detachment and contempt, was born hollow. That was my father,' he said and he stopped again at this point. I wondered if, with that, the carnage had come to an end, but I soon discovered worse was yet to come.

'My father killed my mother,' he said a few moments later, 'at least I think he did.' And then he burst into floods of tears.

You think he did? I thought, as I sat facing him.

He was racked with sobs. I worried, I admit, about the bone china that shook in his hands, the teacup rattling on the saucer. I could do nothing to comfort him, I couldn't reach out my hand even, because I realised I was terrified.

Finally the crying subsided and he sat forward in his chair and I am happy to say he delivered the crockery onto the relative safety of the coffee table that stood between us. He pulled in a huge lungful of air and rolled his head back so that he was looking up at the ceiling, and as he exhaled he sat forward in his chair and looked at me. I ascertained by the look on his face that he felt he had been discovered. I wanted to assure him that nothing was further from the truth. He remained a complete mystery to me.

'Drink your tea,' he said as he stood up.

There was a crimson red box with gold trim on the corner of the sideboard. He pulled a number of tissues through a slit in the top of it. I thought for a moment of him buying the box, and I imagined him placing it over his plain box of man-size tissues and I was afraid for a moment that I would laugh.

When he blew his nose he sounded like a car horn.

Finally he turned round and I truly saw him for the first time. His velvet smoking jacket was a size too small for him. He looked slightly ridiculous in his fluffy teddy carpet slippers; the cuddly face on the front was leering at me, its mouth stretched wide as he flexed his toes. He sat back down. When he picked up the cup and saucer his hands looked as if they might crush the delicate pottery. He suddenly seemed to have the beginnings of a vulpine beard. His red-rimmed eyes had become steely blue and the lines on his forehead were deep and met in a deeply-etched v between his eyebrows, which in turn were overgrown and unkempt. His lips were turned up into an ugly sneer, revealing his yellowing teeth, which had been sharpened to points.

I feared for myself, I admit it, I didn't fear for his descendants. (But of course he had never married and he vowed he never would. This was part of his plan. I imagined he thought himself a dam, behind which all this was straining; he stood with his back against it.)

He took a sip of his tea and there followed a momentary battle within him; I watched as he tried to pull himself together. Then slowly, as the infusion of leaves began their work, his hands regained their previous deftness of touch and the murderous look in his eyes became diffused, as if diluted by the brew. His grimace turned into a smile.

He fell silent, he only watched me over the rim of his cup as he sipped at his tea. It occurred to me at that moment, and for the hundredth time during that meeting, that my tea was poisoned. I admit I had thought it throughout the conversation, I can't properly tell you when it first came to me. It had also occurred to me that Walter had already been dispatched in the same way and I felt a touch of remorse as well as fear. I could hear a low moan. It was coming from me. Mr D cocked his head to one side and listened.

To whom it may concern: is there anybody out there listening?

Although I have warned you about Mr D, nothing has been done. I have only just made it back to my room; I have been wandering around in the corridors for what seems like hours.

I feel I have been spared like the man in the dormitory; I feel close to death. It is only a feeling, but it is all-pervasive. It soaks into my bones.

Listen, he has seen through me. Otherwise why would he let me in on the truth that he is from a family of cold-blooded killers? Yes, he was playing with me. He told me fully in the knowledge that he had found me out as a letter writer and a betrayer of Walter's trust. But I did not know I was found out until it was too late, because all the while he had been feeding me poisoned tea. (How am I supposed to know what it tastes like when all the brews he gives me are weird tasting?)

When he got up and excused himself – 'All this tea has made me want to pee, I won't be a minute' – he was probably thinking: When I return I'll finish off the job; suffocation with the tea cosy or a jab to the throat with the handle end of the teaspoon, but I was wise to it and I slipped out while I still could, although I hardly could; I was hot with a fever and my legs were weakened. I made sure he couldn't find me. And then I was lost. After I had wandered around for some time, in a delirious fever, I finally made it back to my room.

The thing is though, if I am found dead in the morning it is him who has done it.

I have been poisoned. I am sure of it. Help. I might survive if I can make it through the night.

Now I am in a panic because he might come and finish me off anyway. Does he know where I am? If he does, I am done for. I am too tired to move. Did he ever visit Walter? He has never visited me. Maybe he doesn't know where I am. Maybe I am safe here.

I did wake up and when I did there was a man sitting on the chair by my bed.

Although we shared the room for a while, a half-hour or so, he didn't speak to me. In fact, he didn't even look at me.

In the end I simply left him, and in the evening when I returned he was still there.

At the time I didn't understand the repercussions his arrival was going to have for me.

First of all though, let me tell you how I felt that first morning.

'Who are you?' I asked him after a few minutes of silence had passed. I was still sitting up in my bed. But as I've already told you, he didn't speak.

'How did you get into my room?'

Still nothing, of course.

I quickly left after that. I admit I was frightened of him, the fear I had felt of Mr D the night before was washed away with the fear I had of this stranger. And for the whole day I worried that I would have to return and find he was still there. I stayed away later than I normally would have.

Now let me tell you what happened when I returned in the

evening. I hoped that he had gone as he had arrived; just as he'd had the whole night to appear in, I had given him the whole day to reverse the trick. I might even have offered up a few words to god as I stood outside the door, a gesture of some sort, not a gesture, a request more like, with the promise of something from me in return, I don't know, eternal felicity or something. Anyway I suspected even then it would all come to nought, I'd never been acknowledged in any way prior to this and I saw no reason for a change in the divine policy for my benefit at this point.

When I opened the door I saw the back of him, and I saw he still hadn't moved, perhaps he was sitting slightly more askew, but only slightly. The back of his skull was impenetrable. His hair was cut to a very short black stubble. His ears stuck out from his head, I could see the light through the thin gristle. It looked as if his head had caught fire and was still smouldering at the ears. Apart from that I could see he was wearing a grey jacket, and a thin strip of his white shirt showed above his jacket collar. That was all I could see from my position at the door.

After a few minutes considering my situation I walked quickly over to the bed and sat on it. I was facing him. We mirrored each other, our hands on our knees. I looked for a suitable expression to indicate that my intention was to face it out.

I said, 'I'm in my element here, you bastard. I can sit it out with the best of them.'

I immediately regretted having said anything. I felt I had, by speaking, passed a small advantage to him. I had indicated that he had me rattled, while he remained largely, no, he was wholly unaffected by it all, the fucker.

Yes, he definitely has you rattled, the mutinous voice in my head was saying to me, *he's got you on the run.* Shut up! I said to myself, the voice loyal to me said to myself. I shall counter him by staring past him and making my eyes glassy, what about that? *Can't you see this man is a professional,* the voice comes back at me; *it's going to take something a little more impressive than a glassy eye or two.* Be quiet!

But although I started my countering in earnest, my glancing past him with the glassy eyes, I almost immediately began to peek at him out of the corner of my eye to see how he was being affected by my new offensive strategy. He hadn't flinched, he was like a lump of rock, whereas my eyes were flicking backwards and forwards, a moment of looking glassy-eyed and then following that a quick glance to see if he had noticed. And because my mind was working overtime, at the same rate as my eyes, thoughts flicking in it this way and that, it didn't take long for it to occur to me what my problem was. My problem was I had nothing to get hold of. I had nothing to chase down. In effect I had nothing to counter against. To all intents and purposes, in fact, I was countering against a brick wall.

At that moment I felt somewhere in me that my position was untenable. I was lost. But I didn't allow this notion to come to the surface. I concentrated on my unbeaten record at this kind of stand-off, and continued countering in earnest.

Within twenty minutes though I was sweating, my eye was twitching, now completely of its own accord, my fingertips were unconsciously beating a tune on my thigh so I almost began whistling along to it.

I was itching all over.

I was allowing my mind to wander without maintaining any of the necessary focus; I was dreaming of a day in the Dordogne, or a boat trip up the Dardanelles, or a Christmas in Dorset, I was anywhere but here. And yet he had not moved, he had not spoken either, the fucker.

Suddenly I couldn't bear it any longer, and before I was able to stop myself, I rose quickly to my feet, in fact I almost leapt into the air.

'You bastard!' I shouted at him.

But even this had no effect on him. He remained immovable.

I began to pace the cell, not as a means of undermining him, all of that kind of thing was gone out of the window by now, no, I was impelled to do it by my own self, because physically I knew I couldn't sit or stand still any longer, my body knew it by itself, and without instruction from the head it set to pacing backwards and forwards.

And I thought I was howling, but whatever it was, the tears were pouring out of me. He had moved something in me. I struggled for breath.

He sat motionless. He sucked all the air out of the room.

In the end I lay on the bed, curled up, my back facing towards him. I lay like this until the light faded, became almost solid and began its retreat across the room towards the window. But it wasn't a time to relax, and that's not what I was doing. Lying still was agony, but I felt it was the right thing to do. I had gotten hold of myself again by this point and was thinking of ways to limit the damage.

Whereas before – when I was largely confident I would be victorious in the stand-off against him and only a small part deep in me knew that the situation was lost – now the thing was reversed, and a large part of me knew it was lost, but there remained deep in me some slight sniff of victory. This was why I was thinking of ways to limit the damage, even now, because of that slight flame of hope still burning. It seems pathetic when I look back on it.

Anyway, when I turned over to face him I saw that he was still there, but I became convinced he had moved – his hand, his head – and this was a small victory.

I slept fitfully. I had a dream that I thought was true. At some point it began to break down and it turned out he was only a man and the route was full of obstacles that I couldn't surmount unless I put them from my mind. This was a mixture of dreaming and being half awake, all the time aware of him still in the room.

Anyway, somehow I stepped into the dream; I strode in over the white cobbles. I listened to what I was thinking, and while I might have been trying to speak in the dream, the words didn't come out of my mouth into the world of the dream, or into the room outside of it either, instead there was a pocket that was somehow touching the day, it was a rent in the dream, like a pocket is a split in a trouser leg, but it properly touched neither the dream within nor the room without.

The next morning I didn't bother showering as usual, or eating breakfast, I just had to get out of there. I headed for the light.

I made for the day room.

The sun hadn't come over the roof yet, and the air in the day room was somewhat greyer, but nevertheless the windows and the white walls made the place unforgiving; nothing could hide safely in there.

I sat down in a spot that afforded me a view of the whole room, but I wasn't looking for anybody in particular; anyway, at this time of the morning, the room was empty.

I considered my situation. I wanted to make some notes but I had left my pen behind.

There was a man in my room.

I didn't know who he was. I considered the run of events that had brought me to this point. When he had first appeared in my room, and while I still had it in my mind that in the end I would be able to better him in the stand-off, I was at least comfortable. It's easy to say this with hindsight, but now it was too late. I was out the other side, and the stand-off, as a last resort, was behind me. What is there to do when the last resort is behind you?

Nothing.

I was at the end I was certainly at the end then.

So I began to rue my decision to rush into the stand-off at such an early stage of the proceedings, but I also began to think – because I was always looking for something to salvage from the situation – I thought, maybe I can live with him there in the room. Yes, I decided, in time I would come to see him as no more important than the table or the sink or the bed. Of course I would not be able to sit on the chair and this would be a nuisance, but something I would be able to live with nonetheless, and of course I wouldn't be able to sit at the desk, or sit anywhere else in the room for that matter, but even this, I thought, would be surmountable, I would surely find another private place to sit when I felt the need to sit; and in the end, as he became nothing more than another piece of the furniture, I might decide it was safe to sit on my bed after all, with him in the room, without too much bother, or I could sit on his knee as if he were a part of the chair.

This of course was all hypothetical, because I had driven myself out of the room.

I had to find the courage to go back.

The day room started to fill up around me. Some fool told me I was sitting on his chair. I told him there were a hundred other chairs. He looked crestfallen of course, after all this was his chair, but I was determined to hold my ground and so I set myself for another stand-off: I found though, that I was too weak, I knew I wasn't up to it, the stand-off with the man in my room had done for me. Luckily though, the man was a fool, as I said, and he didn't see this and wandered off before the stand-off even properly began.

I sat there mourning the loss of my powers.

Some other man to the side of me was waving as if he was on some ocean liner and his wife was on the dock. I'd have felt sorry for him, but for the fact he had an enormous grin on his face. Was he happy though, I thought, or was he merely putting a brave face on it for the benefit of the people he was leaving behind?

After I had been sitting there for about an hour, I decided to go and get something to eat. I was still in time for breakfast because I had risen so early. I thought about a fried egg with beans and mushrooms and blood pudding and coffee, and realised my hunger hadn't suffered unduly under the circumstances. Thank god for small mercies, I thought.

As I got up to leave, I saw the man whose seat I had taken shuffling on his second-choice chair across to my right, and then he paused momentarily, on the edge of his seat, until he thought I was far enough away to give him a good chance to get to the chair before I could if I changed my mind and turned back, and then he rose quickly and scurried across to sit where I had been sitting. I didn't turn back though because I knew, even without looking at him, that he had that look on his face that suggested he thought somehow he had been victorious, as if there had, after all, been some kind of stand-off taking place between us, but a stand-off held at a safe distance, and he had won it. But this was the sort of stand-off I didn't hold with, the kind of stand-off that could be mistaken for something else, that could easily be mistaken for sitting down and looking at the view.

The canteen was almost empty when I got there. As soon as I found myself in front of the egg and bacon and sausages though, I discovered my hunger for meat had left me after all. I settled for toast and tea. I sat there dipping the former in the latter because there was no butter.

I considered my situation some more. Previous to this moment I had thought exactly this: there's a man in my room and I have no idea where he has come from. I had already tried to make a mental list of all the possible reasons for his presence, but so far I hadn't got very far with it. First of all I had toyed with the idea that he might be X, after all wasn't it X I been sent here to meet?

But even as this idea had come in to my head, I dismissed it. I still had my case outstanding, after all, and I had been told to await further instructions. I decided X would wait until the whole thing was untangled before putting in an appearance.

Having discounted X as a possibility, I immediately became lost for further ideas.

As I chewed on my toast it occurred to me that I might wait for him to eat; I could watch him leave from some secluded spot in the corridor, wait for my room to become empty again. It might even be possible to reclaim the room, if I wedged the chair against the door handle and was more careful in future not to leave it unattended.

Secretly I was in mourning for the loss of my morning ritual, ugly as it had become. This is what I did, up until yesterday: I'd wake up half an hour before breakfast, stretch, and then go to the washroom to shower, to shit and to shave, and without fail every day when I looked at myself in the shower-room mirror, I recognised myself less and less. I thought myself haggard and lacking in colour; to all intents and purposes, I thought, the eyes are dead. This was always my first disappointment of the day. Then I sat on the john and inevitably found it difficult to shit, my bowel was lethargic, I think because my heart simply wasn't in it, and this, I suppose, was my second disappointment of the day.

I steeled myself for the disappointments to come before showering, towelling myself dry and returning to my room. I pushed the bed against the door and sat down at the table. The table rocked with the slight pressure I applied as I placed my hands on the desktop and I always thought, every morning, about wedging something under one of the legs; and then I always said to myself, it's too late for that now, do it after, while at the same time acknowledging the voice in my head that told me in that same moment it wouldn't get done afterwards either, so it never got done. Certainly, now it would never get done and this was almost the hardest thing of all to bear.

I concentrated instead on letting my breath settle and my body become still and when I was satisfied and was almost holding my breath, I closed my eyes and made my mind a blank. My body was still sensitised enough from the hot shower to feel the air moving around outside it.

For five minutes every morning I escaped in this way.

And while I remained in this state, I thought, if I have my eyes closed nobody will see me. I closed my eyes.

So there you go.

When I saw Mr D coming in I couldn't stop myself calling out to him as if he was an old friend, it was involuntary, like a reflex action. He waved back as an old friend would, and when he had got his fry-up he came and sat down across from me.

Anyway, I thought, never mind, the trick now is not to let him know that I know he has been poisoning me, to make all the right noises, to try and show him that nothing has changed between us – yes, that was the way I'd do it.

'What happened to you last night?' he asked.

'Never mind,' I said, 'when I woke up there was a man sitting by my bed.'

'What?' he asked.

'Are you listening to me?'

'Who was it?'

'How do I know?'

He told me he was certain it was an incoming man. He said, 'The incoming men are arriving today.'

'Today?'

'Yes. He's definitely a "rogue" incoming man who's arrived early and, it seems, under his own steam.'

Yes, I thought, yes.

'Somehow there's been an administrative error, and he's ended up in your room by mistake.'

Yes.

He took a sheet of paper out of his pocket where he had stuffed it. 'This is a programme of the convention events,' he said.

'Where did you get it?' I asked.

'They're in the foyer,' he said. 'I stole one.'

It was made up of a single sheet folded into two (effectively creating a four-page booklet), and it was set out as you might expect of a programme: the title on the front: 'Incoming Men Convention and Associated Activities'. Inside there were the names of the conference speakers – and each was qualified by letters and numbers after their names, and also their fields of expertise, as well as the times of their slots.

Some of the lectures had titles, or a small piece of descriptive writing obviously designed to attract the attention. One was titled: 'The Importance of Public Relations – How to Manage Your Outgoing Man'. Another more obscure example said something like: 'The institution x, in x, which is currently under observation, embarked upon a radical programme that included an enforced period of fasting, bizarre night-time exercises in the forest and a three-hour session every day intoning a single word allocated upon entrance to the institution. Failure to submit to these simple disciplines was punishable by a prolonged period standing in the sun.'

There was a lecture on 'Achieving a place on "the heightened plane", by learning from successive appointments – and the use of the accrued knowledge in the furthering of this aim'.

I put the programme on the table in front of me. Mr D was busy eating.

'Why are you trying to kill me?' I asked him, suddenly. I took myself by surprise. I hadn't meant to say it.

'What?' he asked.

'Did you kill Walter?' I asked him.

'Are you mad?' he said.

I instinctively held the square of toast up against my face and from my position of cover I was able to watch him finish off his breakfast.

I sat in the canteen after he had gone, until they asked me to leave and then I went for a walk in the grounds. I sat on a bench by the pond. I could hear someone smashing tennis balls. People cried out and cheered in equal measure after every shot. The woman I had seen before was feeding the ducks again. A man stopped in front of me to tie his shoelaces.

Meanwhile I saw and heard everything.

I wandered aimlessly around corridors and rooms. The rest of the building, beyond my room Walter's room Mr D's room the canteen and the day room had always been a mystery to me.

I had walked always with a purpose, except following Walter's disappearance when I was lost

but if I was lost it was because I paid no attention to where I was wandering; in truth I was never lost

the world was finite

I need only walk until I came to a dead end and then turn around

sooner or later I would arrive back in the centre of things.

From one window a few floors up, I must have been at the front of the building, I saw the incoming men arriving

a number of buses pulled up   they swept into the car park one by one, appearing from behind the high wall that ran around the whole building.

I couldn't hear the buses myself, a few birds rose up into the air to announce their arrival.

The windows of the buses were dark. I could only make out movement inside

luggage was piled up on the Tarmac

people came out from the building from under me to greet them

Finally, groups of men in grey suits – say, thirty or thirty-five for each bus – got off and blinked in the light

Having ended up with my face pressed up against the glass I turned around and walked back the way I had come

After walking for what seemed like hours, I suddenly found myself in the corridor outside my room.

How had I got here?

I stood there frozen, in a state of confusion, long enough for the lights to turn themselves off over my head.

When I opened the door I saw the man was still there, but now he was on his hands and knees at the foot of the bed. The chair he had been sitting on was overturned and lay slightly under the table. Other than that the place was recognisably the place I had left that morning.

It fleetingly came into my head that if I had the mind to, I could make it to the chair first, and turn it upright and sit on it and this gave me the strength to walk into the room.

I stood over him. I thought, the last time I made the mistake of sitting down.   This way I believed I could maintain some sort of edge.

I was suddenly aware that he wasn't such a big man, especially because he was on the floor, and because he was on his hands and knees I suppose. I could clearly see the soles of his shoes

> they looked to me to be untouched. I
> thought, this man hasn't even been to the end of
> the road.

In a faltering voice I asked him if he had any instructions for me

but he still wasn't giving anything up.

I want you to consider the ludicrousness of the situation for a moment:

I ended up with my hands in the side pockets of his
jacket and then taking them out empty a moment
later

before almost grappling with him to look for the
envelope in the inside jacket pocket.

I stood astride him and reached round from the back as if I
was embracing him   it was quite a sight

And he might have been fighting me or maybe I was tickling
him, I don't know. Anyway there it was. When I stood up again
I had nothing in my hand; I had hoped, I think, to find
something because I had taken this route and it was another
step on a path that was becoming irreversible.

I instinctively picked up my case   I was probably in a
panic and I put it on the bed.

I quickly packed my few shirts and underwear and the clock.
I thought he could have the soap and the deodorant. I closed
the case.   The light was already closing in   the days are
getting shorter I said to myself

but somehow it only enabled me to see things
clearer, the black and white of the dusk light clarified
everything

and I could hear everything so much better as well

things like the tap dripping   and under that the
sound of his shallow breathing

                    I thought

                            he's looking to

conserve his air.

By now I had my back to him I moved the case from my left
hand to my right hand yes I said without any true conviction

                        other than that I

                   let

the pictures drift across my mind

                    I was very aware that the world
was a big place   I had a picture of it in my head and I
imagined that I would stop walking

                      further to this I was at a
loss as to what I should do.

Even then before I stepped outside I thought, I could have sat
on the chair   it had been a decision

                  I chose to be thrust out into

          something else

What else could I have done?

What did I do?

I was humming with conviction or was it the idea of
conviction?

I thought, I'll go into the town   then I thought, would I be allowed to go into the town? First though I thought

I'll go to the day room. I decided to return to the day room.

The day room was full. The day room was full mostly of incoming men. The curtains had been drawn and the fluorescents were on, casting a very even and dead light over everything

that was only punctuated when a match flared up or a lighter

All the preparations for the Incoming Men's Ball were done with. It was still early in the evening but the dance band were already on the stage warming up.

I stood on the edge of the dance floor and put my case on the floor by my side. There was a woman alone in the middle of the floor .　　Colubrine.　　It was Colubrine

wasn't it?

yes

She was dancing. Yes, it was Colubrine dancing then

she had her arms out in front of her as if she was clutching a partner　　one rigid the other bent into an arc her hand cupping the small of an invisible back.

She had become something else meanwhile, since I had last seen her　　she was bigger　　tauter somehow, in every good way

A few of the men stood with their backs to the walls looking at her with glassy eyes   they longed to find in themselves

                            a feeling

that had been lost

She was glorious to look at, moving, to her left, slowly, lightly, on her tiptoes, in a great wide circle.

There were men playing dominoes and chess. There were pockets of incoming men sitting together   people sat by warily, watching them.

Walter, meanwhile, was sitting alone in the corner.

Walter!

Walter, is it really you?

I wondered if I was dreaming but I couldn't have been. I could clearly see Walter   his face was impassive, if he was looking at Colubrine he wasn't letting her know that he remembered their dance together

        Walter   I wanted to sit with him, I wanted to sit with Walter

        but I found I wasn't able to step onto the floor. I was in

        too

fragile a state to risk any kind of encounter with Colubrine, even a nod or worse still a word, and yet she was between me and Walter

                her and the vast dance floor.

For a good ten minutes then I stood on the carpet surrounding the floor   I was standing fearfully   a non-swimmer on the edge of a swimming pool.

Colubrine paid me no heed as she swept past me time and time again, every few minutes, with her eyes closed.

I suppose in that time my mind also drifted   and so it took a while for me to realise that some of the men standing around the edge of the room had begun to look at me with the same glassy eyes that they had been using on Colubrine.

I had been drawn into some kind of encounter without realising it.

The metres between Colubrine and me had become charged with some kind of tension.

She swept past me again with her eyes closed.

No, it was all in the eyes of the men I said to myself. But the longer I couldn't move the more involved I became, for them, the observers: the more sensitised they became to the potential for action and in the end the whole room was infected with

it   :

men turned away from watching the incoming men

the incoming men turned away from their conversations with other incoming men

more men turned away from their game of dominoes

another sacrificed his queen to get a better look

I remained stricken   I couldn't move

I thought, she'll have made another full rotation soon enough
she'll open her eyes soon enough and I shall be face to face with
her.

I looked for Walter   I longed for him to call out
and save me.   Walter!   If he could
call out I would be saved

                    the spell would be broken. Colubrine
made another pass. I looked inside myself for strength

               breathe

and in that moment when you are most full of air find
some reserve

          stretch out the first leg and the other will follow. But I
was exhausted of all residual energy.

At this point I began to   disengage with myself
               I became two
                    This is how I did it:
               in the out breath I was spent and stood on
               the edge of the black hole
                    – I gave myself up to inevitabilities that were
               not of my choosing
               this was the part of me into which
               she
               when she was facing me   and was looking at

me

  would find no comfort

And on the next intake of breath   some other part
of me stepped into the air.   And
I strode over to Walter   neither above the floor nor on it.

He looked at me as I approached him. That's a good sign, I
thought. But then I saw that he had not seen me at all, he only
looked, dead-eyed, out into the room. He couldn't see
Colubrine dancing either.

'What happened to you?' I asked him

(– he had been inexplicably moved
I imagined him in his new room   on an undisclosed floor
    at an undisclosed hour
and it had been impossible to find him again ,   I told him
this   I told him I had been feeling disoriented
  we are living in what seems to be different universes
    I said   and then I told him my circumstances were very
much altered it seemed my past has been lost to me
  and my present was being made even as we spoke –)
I told him I was sorry

Meanwhile Colubrine was forever growing or I was getting
smaller

or on the out breath

               another few moments were lost to me

Walter's pills were in a line on the tray that was in front of
him on the tabletop   they were made of a hundred colours

He sat back slightly

      but in the doing of the action his head didn't tilt back it
swivelled forward on the neck

               so that he continued to face me

  it was just a slight arching of his back ,that opened up his
chest and lifted his shoulders up   and back

I was overcome by a wave of sadness. There was suddenly a
glimpse of something in his eyes, whatever was left of him was
kicking around   his eyes were blinking on and off like a
strip-light coming on in the belly of a house. I watched him
struggle with himself. I wondered if he sensed that I was there.

Then I saw the pills were not in a straight line and I couldn't
take my eyes off them. They rolled this way and that because
he couldn't keep his hands still. They didn't fall on the floor
because the lip of the tray surrounding them prevented it

    instead they were returned into the field of play. He closed
his eyes and when he opened them again I saw that he was lucid
if you like he fixed his gaze on something over my shoulder

He picked up one of his pills and dropped it into the glass of water

    'What are you doing?' I asked, but he didn't hear me

        we both watched it sink to the bottom   it moved
ever so slightly back and forth as if it weighed nothing
         I thought   those can't be tidal waters
         I thought   it's the friction of the tablet entering
        water   that has set up some kind of squall.
I waited for the pill   to sit still.

    In that same moment   as all the possibilities opened up
before me   Colubrine opened her eyes
    and looked at me   and what had been the husk of
  me   that was left behind on the edge of the dance
  floor   was swallowed up
I was only aware that I could never move from here
             the walls
           folded
in around me
    in my eyes there were blackened-out holes
        before she took
me in her arms like an empty set of clothes and carried me
with her   I continued to stare at Walter

        on the in breath   I found that

I

was unable to breathe out

                                as the air leaked in through my nose I could

feel myself expanding into something else

   Walter brushed his arm across the tray and scattered the

tablets they bounced and rolled onto the dance floor

   There was a moment of heavy silence the sort of silence you

could measure other silences against

            then the pill suddenly began to fizz in the water

air bubbles rose rapidly to the surface

                                    where they sat for a second

                    and

   then popped

              and then I could hear the dance music

                            booming in my

                    head

     before Colubrine was almost upon us

   her back coming towards us

           and turning away from us

                          at the same

     time

   we sat for a moment   waiting.

 doors were opening up and closing inside of me